BURIED BIKER

THE JESSE DAMON SERIES

BURIED BIKER

KM ROCKWOOD

A Jesse Damon Crime Novel

WILDSIDE PRESS

*To Ringo
and his riding buddies.*

Published by Wildside Press LLC
www.wildsidepress.com

CHAPTER 1

As I walked home, I turned the corner and saw a car sitting in the alley. A black Lincoln Town Car—much too classy and sedate for this neighborhood—was idling just past the stairs that led to my basement apartment.

Cops?

Cars that have been seized in drug arrests are often put to use for police surveillance, and a couple of the detectives who liked to keep a close eye on me had a real taste for luxury sedans.

I rubbed my stubbly cheek with my hand. I needed a shave. *Was it too late to turn around and go the other way? Probably.*

I kept my hands out of my jacket pockets and let them hang by my sides, in full sight. No point in giving them any reason to think I might be reaching for a concealed weapon. I'd never been Tased, but I'd seen it done to people, and I had no desire to experience it firsthand.

Maybe they aren't waiting for me. Maybe I can make it into my apartment before they saw me.

Maybe the sun won't rise tomorrow morning.

The wind whipped up a rumpled plastic bag in the street, blowing it over the curb and against the worn bricks of the building. I reached the stairs that led from the sidewalk down to my apartment and grasped the handrail which was slick with frozen rain. A car door slammed.

A gravelly voice sounded behind me. "Jesse Damon. Stop."

Damn. Detective Belkins. Montgomery, his partner, wouldn't be far behind.

"Put your hands on top of your head. Interlace your fingers. Step back toward me. Slowly."

The wet spots on the sidewalk were beginning to freeze, making the footing treacherous. Since I was backing up, I couldn't see where I was going. When I got a few feet back from the stairs, even with the front of the car, Montgomery said, "Lean on the front of the car."

The alley light glared on the hood of the car. I turned and put my palms down on it. I spread my feet and leaned my weight onto my hands.

From beside me, Belkins kicked my unresisting foot back further. I smothered a grin. I was wearing steel-toed work boots, and he favored worn loafers. Limping slightly, he stepped to the side of the car, so I could just see him out of the corner of my eye. Belkins wore a wrinkled trench coat and held an unlit cigar clenched in his teeth.

His partner, Detective Montgomery, stepped up behind me. "You got anything on you I should know about?"

"No, sir." I was on parole, and they didn't need a warrant, probable cause, or any reason at all to search me or my apartment. Having anything illegal or dangerous, even a box cutter from work, could be grounds for violation. I'd be on a quick trip to jail to await a violation hearing.

Montgomery leaned in close behind me. I could smell his aftershave and minty mouthwash. He swung into the usual routine, his dark manicured hands sweeping under my jacket, between my legs and into my pockets. He deposited my wallet and key on the hood of the car in front of me. This whole humiliating routine was getting pretty old to me, but they never seemed tire of it.

Montgomery grabbed one of my hands and pulled it behind me, turned the palm outward and snapped on handcuffs. He did the same with my other hand, but when I tried to straighten up, he leaned against my shoulder, leaving me leaning forward awkwardly. I knew better than to force the issue.

"Just want to ask you a few questions, Jesse." His voice was slow, and he was making an effort to sound nonthreatening.

My stomach cramped. They were going to play good cop/bad cop. They were good at it. If I gave them a hard time, they'd report that I wasn't being cooperative to Mr. Ramirez, my parole officer. Who would, as usual, ask me what I had to hide and remind me that I had years of backup time if he decided to send me back to prison. Like that wasn't totally in my mind every waking moment.

Belkins took the cigar out of his mouth and spit on the pavement. "So you still on parole, Damon?"

"Yes, sir." He knew that. He was just playing with me.

"They still haven't fired you yet from that job?"

"No." I wasn't about to lose that job if I could help it. I'd really lucked out, getting hired on as a laborer at a steel fabrication plant, and I knew I'd never get another job that good if I lost it. I worked hard, and I'd been promoted to forklift driver.

Montgomery took over. "So how's that girlfriend of yours, Jesse?"

"Kelly? She's not really my girlfriend." I wished she was. We worked the overnight shift at Quality Steel Fabrications, both driving forklifts. I was mostly assigned to the warehouse and the production floor, while she loaded and unloaded trucks in the shipping room, but there was a lot of overlap in our responsibilities. Sometimes we saw each other outside work, mostly over at her house. Fix dinner for her two kids, play games with them, watch TV. Then, after they went to bed, we'd follow suit in her big soft bed. I'd been locked up since I was a kid, and she'd introduced me to sex. With her, it was even better than I had ever imagined. Her ample, muscled body curved in all the right places, she was divorced, and she treated me like a regular person, not a paroled convict.

But we both had a lot of issues and knew we weren't in a position to make commitments. Especially with her young kids involved. Their lives so far hadn't been exactly ideal. I'd spent most of my childhood in foster care, being pulled out of relationships with adults just as they were getting comfortable, and I didn't want to do that to any kids. Realistically, how long would it be before I got locked up again?

Belkins gave me a shove.

I must have missed a question.

Montgomery asked, "I said, when'd you see her last?"

"Thursday night at work."

"Thursday night? I thought you worked the early morning hours."

"Yeah. I guess you're right. Friday morning."

"Like, this morning?"

"Yeah." I'd caught a few hours of sleep, and it seemed a lot longer ago than that. It is easy to get all mixed up when they throw questions around like that. Of course, that was one of the main reasons they kept doing it. They'd twist the words against me and throw them back at me. I'd say something stupid and contradictory, giving them more ammunition.

"Haven't seen her since you got off from work?"

"No, sir."

"Why's that?"

Why indeed? But I said, "Her dad just got out of prison. She let him use her place on his home plan. I'm on parole."

"And?"

"I'm not supposed to associate with convicted felons. So I can't go over to her place when he's around."

"Why don't you have her over here at your place?"

I shrugged.

Belkins said, "Because it's a rat hole, and you don't want her over here?"

He was right. It *was* a rat hole, but that wasn't the main reason. "I only got the one room. She's got two kids. Not a good place to bring them."

He laughed. "First believable thing you've said in a long time."

Montgomery took over again. "Where were you this afternoon, Jesse?"

"Washed my clothes at the Laundromat. Then I went to the library just before it closed, for a few books. Went out a little later to get something to eat off the McDonald's dollar menu. That's where I'm coming from now."

Belkins snorted. "The library? I thought you had to be able to *read* to go to the library."

Montgomery chuckled. "I don't think that's entirely true, from some of the people I've seen hanging around in there. But Jesse's not stupid. He can read."

"So you haven't seen Kelly all day?" Belkins asked.

"Not since we got off work."

"So it wasn't you beat the crap out of her?"

My throat closed, and I couldn't breathe. I jerked upright, turning to face Belkins. "What?" I managed to say.

Montgomery grabbed me by the back of the neck, slamming me face-first onto the hood. "Don't make any sudden moves."

Licking blood off my lower lip, I forced myself to remain still, my muscles tensed.

One hand tight on my neck and the other on my arm, Montgomery said, "Settle down. I don't want to have to hurt you."

He already *was* hurting me, but not seriously. Taking a deep breath, I willed my body to relax. My nose crushed into the cold, wet surface of the car's hood. I asked, "Is she okay?" Even to me, my voice sounded strangled.

"Good question." Montgomery's hand felt heavy on the back of my neck. "In the hospital right now. Hasn't regained consciousness. Time will tell."

I was bent at the waist, leaning forward onto the hood of the car. The muscles in my back were starting to cramp, and blood was puddling around my nose and mouth. I closed my eyes and asked, "Is she going to be all right?"

No one answered. The silence stretched on. I took a few deep breaths and tried to ease the strain in my back by shifting one foot.

Montgomery's grip tightened. "Can I let you up?" he asked.

"Yes, sir." It was hard to talk through the pool of blood.

"I have your word for it that you won't try anything?"

"Yes, sir."

Behind us, Belkins snorted again. "You're going to take *his* word for it?"

Montgomery eased up the pressure a little. "We have to let him up sooner or later."

"We can wait for a patrol car to get here," Belkins said. "We're not gonna put him in this car anyhow. We just got it, and it's too nice to mess up."

Montgomery took his hand off my neck anyhow and grabbed my arm. "Stand up."

I was off balance, with my feet still spread behind me, but I stood. Montgomery's grip steadied me.

"Turn around and face me."

I turned. Blood dripped off my chin.

"Look at him." There was disgust in Belkin's voice. "Bleeding like a stuck pig. For sure we're not putting him in this car. He's probably got AIDS or something. You'd better put on rubber gloves."

Montgomery kept his hold on my arm and looked around. "Sit on that curb," he told me, nodding at the edge of the alley behind me. "And cross your legs in front of you."

With his help, I eased to a sitting position and stretched my legs out in front of me, crossing them. It wasn't exactly comfortable, but it beat being bent facedown over the hood of the car. My face was tight, and I felt my nose swelling up.

A few drops of rain splashed on the asphalt, quickly turning into a chilly drizzle. Belkins adjusted his hat so the rain dripped off the back and down the outside of his coat. Montgomery continued to look well put together, as if the weather wouldn't dare interfere with his appearance. I sat on the wet curb, the rain soaking my hair and trickling down my neck, reaching like icy fingers under my jacket.

A million urgent questions boiled up inside me, but I kept them to myself. If they were going to give me any information about Kelly, they would have done so. I tried to concentrate on taking deep breaths through my mouth to steady myself, but sharp pains radiated through my chest. I bit my lower lip. It was already bleeding, so I wasn't going to do much more damage to it. It kept me from screaming at them. I needed to keep my mouth shut.

Montgomery pulled a flashlight from somewhere beneath his impeccable overcoat and shined it in my face. "Look up at me," he commanded.

I closed my eyes and raised my chin.

"Do you need medical attention?" he asked.

"What the hell?" Belkins said. "So he's bleeding. The nurse at the lockup'll take care of it when he's booked."

Montgomery ignored him. "You need to go to the hospital? Your nose looks like it might be broken."

I had pretty good medical insurance from my job that would cover most of the cost. But if I ended up in the emergency room, there'd be record of it. Belkins and Montgomery would have to do some kind of report to account for it. I'd end up with a resisting arrest or, worse, assaulting a police officer charge so Belkins' and Montgomery's asses would be covered.

"No, sir," I said.

"How about an EMT?"

I shook my head.

Siren screaming, a patrol car careened down the street and slammed to a stop next to us. I had to fight an urge to pull my legs in, just in case the car skidded toward me. Two young, uniformed officers scrambled out, one with his gun drawn, the other clutching a Taser.

Belkins moved out of the way. Montgomery stood calmly over me, shielding me from the onslaught.

"Where's the perp?" the cop with the Taser asked.

Montgomery stood his ground. "Right here. I don't think you'll need the weapons."

"Dispatch said 'armed and dangerous,'" the other cop said. "Retaking a paroled violent offender."

"We've got the situation under control for now," Montgomery said. "And you don't want to have to do all the paperwork for use of weapons, do you?"

"Not if we don't have to." The cop holstered his gun.

"You shouldn't have to." Montgomery reached down and took my arm. "Stand up, Jesse."

I lurched to my feet and stood still, trying to look as far from meriting the armed and dangerous designation as possible. I didn't need anyone to get any rougher with me.

The cop still held his Taser, although it was now pointed at the ground. "He's bleeding."

Montgomery glanced at my face. "That's so. You might want to put on gloves."

Both of the uniforms reached for the little pouch on their belts that held rubber gloves. "He's gonna bleed all over the car."

"There are some antiseptic wipes in the trunk of our car," Montgomery said. "Detective Belkins, could you get them for us?"

I thought Belkins was going to refuse, but he bit down hard on his cigar and went to the back of the car, scowling with annoyance. "You want me to get one of them damned teddy bears we got for kids and give it to him, too?"

Montgomery ignored him and turned to me. "Jesse, if I uncuff your hands, will you clean off your face?"

"Okay," I answered.

"And not give anybody any grief?"

"Nope."

He reached behind me and unlocked the handcuffs. I took a few of the proffered wipes and dabbed my mouth and nose with them. They stung and the sharp smell tickled my nose.

"What happened?" one of the uniforms asked.

"We startled him, and he reacted without thinking," Montgomery said. "So I had to slam him down on the car. But I think he's got himself under control now. Don't you, Jesse?"

I looked at the blood-streaked bits of damp paper in my hands and answered, "Yes, sir."

Belkins pulled the cigar out of his mouth and spit on the ground. "Sometimes you're a goddamned idiot, Montgomery. Damon's a murderer. He don't need to be treated like nothing else. Certainly not like somebody who's your goddamned *friend*."

"There are four of us here," Montgomery pointed out. "What's he going to do? You don't understand what makes him tick."

Belkins spit again. "I understand all right. He's a killer. Killers kill. People like him should never be paroled. He should be in prison for life."

I hadn't picked up a life sentence—more like thirty nine years—and Belkins knew it, but I didn't see much point in correcting him.

Montgomery shrugged and turned back to me. "Looks to me like the bleeding's pretty much stopped. Let's get those restraints on again."

One of the uniforms held out a plastic bag and I put the dirty wipes in it. Then I turned around so Montgomery could snap the cuffs back in place.

Another car pulled up and stopped halfway down the block. The driver got out and walked toward us.

Montgomery glanced toward the newcomer. He gestured at the patrol car and said to the cops with the patrol car, "Take him down to Central Booking. Tell them we'll be down in a little while to get him processed."

No one was going to bother to read me Miranda rights. They knew I wouldn't complain. And I knew no one would listen to me if I did.

"Okay." The uniform took me by the arm and propelled me toward the car.

A camera flash went off in my face, temporarily blinding me.

Belkins stepped up next to us. "Hurry it up."

I stumbled. The other uniform, still grasping his Taser, grabbed my other arm and asked, "What charges should I tell them?"

Montgomery shook his head and said, "I'll be right there to take care of it."

But Belkins blurted out, "Rape. Kidnapping. Assault. Attempted murder. That'll do to start."

My gut tightened. *Rape. Kidnapping.* This was *Kelly* they were talking about. I looked pleadingly at Montgomery. I knew he probably wouldn't tell me, but I had to ask. "What happened to her?"

"That," Belkins said, his voice distorted by the cigar he had stuck back in his mouth, "is what we are hoping you will tell us."

CHAPTER 2

Relieved of my belt and boots, I sat on the cold, metal bench in a holding cell at the detention center. Except for the solid steel door, cinderblock walls painted grey surrounded me. The door had a barred hatch near the top which opened from the outside for staff to check on me. There was also a waist high rectangular port, once again opening only from the outside. It was designed to pass meal trays. On the wall opposite the door stood the standard one-piece, all-purpose plumbing unit.

I'd splashed cold water on my face until there were no traces of blood in the sink. When I touched my lip and nose gently, they were swollen, but I didn't think my nose was really broken. No big deal if it was.

For once, I was looking forward to the interrogation I was sure was coming. I knew from experience that Montgomery was a master at extracting information, and he'd gone to great lengths to set himself up as being on my side. He had ignored Belkins' verbal swipes and protected me from possible rough treatment at the hands of the two uniforms who'd been sent to bring me in. He was hoping his payoff would be my cooperation in giving him as much information as I had. Which, in this case, wasn't much at all.

He might very well be right that I'd be willing to cooperate with him. I wanted him to find out who did this to Kelly, and I'd tell him anything I could.

He'd told me just enough about her to make me sick to my stomach and desperate for a chance to learn more. I knew what to expect. To encourage me to talk, he'd divulge selected bits of information that wouldn't compromise the case he was building. I hoped that would include how she was doing, and if she was expected to recover.

I felt the same tightness in my chest I always felt when I knew I was going to be doing this verbal dance with an interrogator. But this time, my stomach clenched, too, and I was afraid I was going to throw up. Usually all I had to do was try to say just enough so nobody could complain to my PO that I was being uncooperative. I'd only been back on the street for a few months, but I'd already realized I was going to be stopped and questioned anytime anything even remotely suspicious happened around me. And it seemed like things happened a lot.

This time, though, if I wanted to get any information back, I'd have to be a more active participant in the game and dangle bits of tantalizing information in front of Montgomery, so he'd tell me about Kelly. That is, if I could manage to *find* any tantalizing bits of information to dangle. And keep my focus well enough not to say anything stupid. Or incriminating.

Montgomery had more experience than I did and was much better at it than I would ever be. Besides, the stakes for him weren't nearly as high.

Keeping me waiting was part of his ploy. It would give me time to get more worried and anxious. If I was particularly unfortunate, they'd keep me in this holding cell for hours. With no windows and lights on 24/7, the only way I'd know how much time passed was by the guard shifts changing every eight hours and the meals that would be delivered.

I couldn't afford to be out of work for long. I was barely making it financially as it was, what with parole expenses, court costs and fines, restitution I owed. All in addition to the usual expenses of living.

Of course, if I ended up with new charges like this anyhow, I wouldn't have to worry about all that. The state would be providing room and board, and nothing else would matter.

I was sure a camera was trained on me, probably linked to both a screen that was monitored in the control room and a recording device.

Sleeping would help pass the time. If I could sleep. Controlling access to sleep would be part of the interrogation process. The more tired I got, the more confused I would be and the more likely to make unguarded statements. Once Montgomery got me out of the cell, he'd also control my access to food and drink. So I should take advantage of any food I was offered. And any opportunity to get some shut eye.

The cell was a small one, not meant to hold anyone for long. The bench was too short for me to lie down on, so I lay on the floor. There was just enough room for me to stretch out if I stuck my feet under the stainless steel one-piece plumbing unit. The floor was cold concrete, but I'd slept in more uncomfortable situations. Like shackled to another inmate on a prison bus as it made its rounds of the state's correctional facilities to transport prisoners.

But I couldn't fall asleep. Every time I closed my eyes, an all-too-vivid image of Kelly rose in my mind. I'd see her with her face battered and her clothes torn, and I couldn't dismiss the picture. What had Belkins said? "Beat the crap out of her"? And Montgomery said she hadn't regained consciousness. They were planning to file rape, kidnapping, and assault charges. *What had happened to her?*

Pressure was building in my chest and my head felt like it was about to explode. I was just coherent enough to recognize the symptoms of being thoroughly traumatized and in a state of panic. Jail cells tended to bring that out in me. No way could I get out of here. Or get any information Montgomery didn't want to give me. I wanted to bang on the walls, shake the bars, scream for someone to tell me what was going on.

That wasn't going to do any good, I reminded myself firmly. Anything like that and I'd find myself restrained. Possibly even medicated, if there happened to be a doctor in the jail at the time. I had to get a grip.

Not able to even keep still, much less sleep, I fell back on the prison coping tactic of doing pushups. It didn't help how I felt a whole lot, but it did keep me from doing something stupid. Maybe it would tire me out, at least physically, so eventually I could fall asleep.

I skipped counting the pushups as I did them and tried to think logically. Unless the forensics lab was totally incompetent, or someone manipulated the report, I should be cleared of any rape charges when the DNA results came in. My DNA was already on file. That, at least, should throw some doubt into the idea that I'd been the assailant.

Or the *only* assailant. Had Kelly been attacked by more than one person? That was an uncomfortable thought.

How long would it take to get the lab results?

Kelly. My gut twisted into a cold knot. *What was going on? Was she going to be all right?*

And why did I care so much? Hadn't I learned over the years that the more I cared about anything, the more I got hurt? Best bet was to not care about anything or anyone. I'd messed this one up, for sure.

I lay my head down on my hands on the floor and was able to doze.

Something clanged into the metal door from the hall and both the upper hatch and the port opened. I propped myself up on my hands and through the port I could see two inmate workers in kitchen whites pushing a cart. A correctional officer trailed them. Meal time. The CO stopped to talk with someone a few feet down the hallway.

I scrambled to my feet.

"So," the short kitchen worker said, smirking as he peered through the bars on the hatch opening. He had to get up on his tiptoes to look in and see me. "We got us a sex offender here, do we? Rape, I hear?"

Amazing how fast information and rumors spread among the inmates in a place like this.

"Shut up, Cappy," the other guy said.

"Screw you, too, Jerome," Cappy said, picking up a filled food tray. He lifted the cover, sniffed the food, and grinned. Then he peered in at me again. "Hungry?" he asked me.

I wasn't, particularly, but I knew I'd eat it all anyhow. I folded my arms in front of my chest and moved up to the hatch so I could see out. I narrowed my eyes and stared at him.

"What happened to your face?" Cappy laughed. "She put up a fight? That why you beat her up, too?"

I stood silently. The door and the bars separated us, and I was well aware that a camera was recording our every move.

"Just give him the damn tray," Jerome said, holding up the cover to the port in the cell door.

Cappy spit on the floor and looked at the tray. "Why should I?"

Was he going to spit in my food?

Jerome glanced down the hallway to where the CO was still talking.

His eyes still on the tray, Cappy said to me, "You got nothing to say for yourself?"

I continued to stare at him. When I did speak, I didn't raise my voice, and he stepped up to the bars in the hatch to listen. "You best hope you're released by the time I hit the general population in this jail."

The tray still in his hands, Cappy stepped back and raised his eyebrows. "Say now, no need for threats. I was just kidding."

"I don't do no kidding. And I don't make no threats. I make *promises.*"

He shifted from one foot to the other, balancing the tray. "You do anything to me, you'll pick up street charges. They got cameras everywhere."

"You think I care?"

"You'll go to prison."

"No place I ain't been before. And where do you think I'm headed now?"

The color drained from his face.

"So if I'm looking at street charges anyhow, when I do catch up with you, I'm thinking I'd best be sure what I give you makes it worth my while," I said.

The CO's voice came down the hallway. "You guys done down there?"

Jerome snatched the tray from Cappy and shoved it through the slot. "It ain't bad," he said to me, his voice quivering. "Meat loaf. And mashed potatoes. One of the better meals."

I didn't move.

Jerome shoved the tray forward a little further into the cell. "Take it," he urged. "Cappy here, he don't mean no harm. Sometimes he got no sense."

The CO came up. "What's taking so long?" he asked.

"Nothing," Jerome said. "Just a few words with the new guy here."

The CO looked at me. I wasn't going to back off from trouble if it sought me out, but I wasn't looking for any, either. Reaching for the tray, I pulled it into the cell. In as normal a voice as I could muster, I said, "Thanks."

Cappy turned and pushed the cart down the hallway, hurrying away from me.

Jerome looked at me and swallowed, his eyes big. "No hard feelings?"

"Nope," I replied.

The CO looked at us and shrugged. He closed the hatch and the port, then checked to make sure they were securely fastened.

All things considered, the meal wasn't bad. If I'd been hungry, it might even have been good. As it was, my stomach was tied in a knot, but I forced myself to eat. No telling when I might get a chance to eat again.

As I was finishing, a CO showed up at the door. "Someone wants to see you," he said.

I put the spoon and empty milk carton in the center of the tray, set it on the bench beside me and stood up. The concrete floor was cold through my socks.

"Door on Holding 2," he said into his radio, and the door slid open. He escorted me down the hallway that smelled of disinfectant , through a grill, and stopped at another door.

"Conference room one," he said into the radio. The door slid open to a small room with bright lighting. There was another door on the opposite wall.

Montgomery was seated at the table in the middle of the room. He gestured at a chair on the other side of the table. I sat. The door slid closed behind me.

Looking around the room, Montgomery said, "This is mostly for lawyers to meet their clients. A lot nicer than the interrogation rooms at the police station, huh?"

I glanced around. It *was* nicer. The walls were painted a soothing blue, and the furniture was clean and in good repair.

He bounced on his chair. "Even got padded chairs," he said.

"True, that." I touched the cushioned seat, then sat on it.

"Now," he said. "Let's get down to business."

"Where's Belkins?" I asked.

He laughed. "We discussed it. He wasn't real happy about it, but we decided it would be better if I conducted this interview by myself. I'm sure I'm not telling you anything you don't know when I say we're being recorded, audio and video. And since the sheriff's department, not the city police, run the detention center, I have no control over what happens to the recordings."

I nodded. More than once Belkins had gotten impatient with my answers and smacked me. Since I was on parole, he knew I wouldn't report it. But then those recordings weren't admissible in court without getting him in trouble. So they just disappeared. Maybe the sheriff's department didn't believe in disappearing tapes.

Belkins was nearing retirement, but Montgomery was an up and coming detective, not about to let questionable evidence taint any case he might take to court. Especially not one that might well end up in a very public trial. He had a sharp eye to what might show up in the newspaper. And we both knew I was pretty newsworthy.

If I picked up another major conviction, I'd be looking at so much time, not to mention the backup time from my previous sentence, I'd have very little incentive to cop a plea. So a trial was likely to be long and well scrutinized. Unless the states attorney decided to make it a capital case. Then I'd have to seriously consider any plea bargain short of execution. An uncomfortable thought, but always a possibility.

"So." Montgomery stretched his long legs out. His grey socks matched his impeccably tailored suit. The overhead light glistened off his highly polished shoes and shaved mahogany head. "Let's talk about Kelly."

I took a deep breath. How much was he going to tell me? "Is she going to be all right?"

He shrugged. "How was she when you left her?"

"She was *fine*. We got out of work, and she said she had to go straight home."

"That's right; you said you had nothing to do with any assault on her."

"It's the truth."

"And the last time you saw her was when you were leaving work."

"Yep."

He leaned forward. "You're not on home detention any more, are you? No ankle bracelet. So nobody was monitoring where you went. Did you follow her home?"

"No. She's got a car. I don't, so I walk. I went to the bank to cash my paycheck, and then I went to my place to get some sleep. Later I went out to run a few errands. And went to McDonald's to get something to eat."

"You know," he said, leaning back in his chair, "I can see how it could happen. She leads you on. You're pretty sure you're gonna get some. Then for whatever reason, she changes her mind. Maybe she makes fun of you. So you get a little mad and take it anyhow."

I just looked at him. "I wouldn't do that. And I wasn't there."

He shrugged. "Any man could understand that. Happens all the time. Just tell me about it."

"*I* wouldn't understand it. Kelly deserves better. *Any* woman deserves better. Wasn't me. How's she doing?" I could hear the quiver in my voice, so I shut up.

Montgomery thought for a minute before he answered. "Physically, she's not too bad. Her shoulder's kind of messed up—dislocated, I think, but not broken. And she's bruised and sore, but no broken bones, no internal injuries that they see."

"Was she unconscious the whole time?"

"I don't think so. The doctor said we had to wait to go talk to her, that they'd given her something to help her sleep, but it got her all agitated, so they gave her something else, mostly for the pain. One of those rape crisis counselors was able to get in there and said she seemed a little calmer, but not what you'd call coherent."

"So she's not in a coma or anything?"

"I don't think so." He straightened the knot on his striped tie. "But she's not really conscious, either. Kind of a restless thrashing around. Which is what they were trying to stop when they gave her the meds that were supposed to put her to sleep."

"Is she's gonna be okay?"

"Psychologically, I don't know. Rape's a hard thing for anyone to get over. Much less rape from someone you know. And maybe trust. She may never be able to trust anybody again." He peered intently at me. "And, of course, she has to really wake up before they'll know if she's got brain damage."

Looking down at the smooth table top and trying to keep any expression off my face, I said, "I didn't rape her. I wouldn't do that."

Montgomery raised his eyebrows. "Rape her, or rape anybody?"

"Rape anybody," I said, holding my voice as steady as I could. "But especially Kelly."

"So if you wouldn't, who would?"

"I dunno." My shoulders tensed. "If I knew, I'd like to…" I let my voice trail off.

"You'd like to what?" Montgomery's keen gaze remained glued to my face.

I forced my muscles to relax. "Nothing," I was going to get myself in real trouble if I wasn't careful.

He leaned back in the chair. "Tell me about this thing you got going with Kelly."

I shrugged. "Not much to tell. We work together, on the same shift."

"And…?"

"And we see each other sometimes. I like her. I guess she must like me some."

"Sleep together?"

"Yeah. When we get the chance."

"Which is how often?"

"I dunno. Was getting to be a regular thing, weekends, but then her dad, Old Buckles, got paroled. She let him use her address for a home plan. She said his bike club's got a place up in the hills, and he'd probably spend most of his time there until he could get a place of his own. But he didn't."

"That put a crimp in things between the two of you?"

"Sure did."

"Suppose he decides to stay living there?"

I shifted uncomfortably. That thought had occurred to me. "Kelly says she don't want it to be a long-term thing. Thinks having him around isn't good for the kids."

Montgomery laughed. "Yet she lets *you* hang around them? How's that good for her kids? You've got a murder conviction."

I was painfully aware of that. "Yeah. But with her dad it's more of a lifestyle thing. He's a real biker. His club, the Predators, hang out a lot. They smoke weed and drink, and do what you'd expect bikers to do, like screw anyone they can in the living room. She don't like that around her kids. And she's worried about maybe losing the house if somebody gets a warrant, and it gets searched and a stash turns up. They can take your house."

"And you two don't do any of that stuff?"

"*I* don't. Kelly drinks a little. But that's legal." More than a little, sometimes. I wasn't going to tell him that.

When I thought about it, I probably shouldn't have said anything about the weed and alcohol. Old Buckles was on parole, too. His was short term, and his bit would be up soon. Not like mine, with years of backup time. But he wouldn't appreciate going back to prison any more than I would.

The weed was of course illegal no matter what, and Kelly's ex was trying to get custody of the kids. I doubted I was telling Montgomery anything he wasn't well aware of, or couldn't find out easily enough. Still, I should have kept my mouth shut.

Montgomery looked thoughtful. "Kelly hang around with the bikers much?"

I shook my head. "Not that I know of. At least not before her dad moved in. But she grew up around them. Her dad raised her. I don't know if she ever rode with them, but she hasn't said much about them since I've known her. And I never saw none of them hanging out around her place."

"Which is how long?"

I closed my eyes and counted back. "Maybe three months since we been seeing each other. I got released about four and a half months ago and started working at Quality Steel right away. That's where I know her from."

"Not long."

"True, that." To me, it seemed like a different lifetime from the one I'd spent in prison.

He shook his head. "You really aren't going to tell me a lot about this, are you?"

"About what? Kelly getting attacked?"

"Yep."

"No, sir. All I know's what you told me."

"Which isn't much."

"Not near as much I'd like to know," I said.

He stood up and stretched. "So what are you going to do about all this?"

I looked up at the scowl on his dark, handsome face. "Me? Not a whole hell of a lot I can do about it. You got me locked up."

"How do you feel about that?"

How did he *think* I felt? "Shitty. If I'm off of work for long, I'm gonna lose my job. And my apartment. Mr. Ramirez is likely to violate my parole and send me back to prison for all my backup time anyhow, even if the charges don't stick. Not to mention that my girlfriend's been beaten and raped."

"I thought you said she *wasn't* you girlfriend?"

"Well, not really. But the closest thing I ever had to a girlfriend."

He ran his fingers over his leg and brushed an imaginary piece of lint off his trousers. "If you do get charged with the rape and assault, do you think they'll stick?"

"They shouldn't. I mean, if they do DNA testing, they'll know it wasn't me. And when Kelly really wakes up, she'll tell you it wasn't me." I refused to entertain the concept that she might *not* regain consciousness. Or that she might have a head injury that would keep her from answering questions intelligently. At the thought, my stomach did a flip.

Montgomery looked toward the door on the other side of the room and straightened his tie. "You really don't know anything about this, do you?"

"No, sir."

"Tell you what," he said, running his hand over his shaved head. "I can't cut you loose. Somebody else—I won't name names, but I think you know who—would just have you picked up again, probably find somebody to issue a retake warrant. It's Saturday now. Let's shelve the new charges until we get a bit more information. Just have you held on parole violation now—I'll get in touch with your PO. Tomorrow's soon enough to bring new charges, if they're going to. Then you can have a bail hearing."

I laughed. "You think I'm gonna get bail set? On these kind of charges?"

Montgomery grinned. "You're probably right about that."

He stepped to the door to summon the CO. "I'll see what I can do," he said. "Just hang tight."

Like I had any choice in the matter.

CHAPTER 3

One of the problems of being on parole was that it would do me no good to complain that a retake warrant hadn't actually been *issued* yet. That would just speed up the process and annoy everyone from the records clerk at the jail to the commissioner who be contacted in the middle of the night to process it.

The mug shots would be useless in a few days when the swelling went down on my face, but they were part of the processing of a new inmate, so the bored clerk took them anyway. Filled out all the forms, took my fingerprints, issued me a bracelet ID. "Twenty bucks to replace that if you lose it," he said, "so try to hang onto it. Leave it on your wrist, and no one can mess with it. Want me to fasten it tight so it don't come off easy?"

"Yeah."

The nurse on duty wasn't gentle as he treated the injuries to my face, but he wasn't unnecessarily rough, either, and I was grateful for that. I endured the standard body cavity search, went through the delousing and shower, and was issued underwear, shower shoes, and a jumpsuit designed for someone three times my size. I wondered when I'd get a chance to shave. Not until tomorrow, if then. No way would I get to use a razor without obnoxiously close supervision.

I shuffled off—no other way to walk in those shower shoes—to be assigned a bunk and issued bedding. It was late, after the nighttime lock-down. The long grey hallway was well lit, but in the housing units that opened off it, the lights were off in the cells and glaring security lights threw grotesque shadows into the corners of the dayroom.

The cells were designed as two-man, but when the place became overcrowded, which tended to happen within months of their construction, they were changed to four-man cells by the simple expedient of moving two sets of double-tiered bunks into each one. Unlike the holding cell, the fronts of the ones here in the housing unit were made of barred grills, open to a central dayroom. A pass-through port for meal trays was in the center of the door. Both were securely locked.

My assignment was K-Pod, the high security cellblock. The cell only had one other occupant, a scared kid who sat nervously on the lower bunk of one set, slapping his shower shoe on the floor. They were the only footwear we'd been issued, and his were so loose they fell off when he tried to lift his foot.

I stowed my bedding on the top of the opposite set of bunks and sat down on the lower one. Pressure was still rising in my chest, and I felt even more like crying or screaming than I had in the holding cell. Then, there'd been some possibility I would be released. Now, I was a processed jail inmate. With no possibility of finding out how Kelly was really doing. I reminded myself that causing a disturbance would just get me restrained and might earn me with an appointment with the psychiatrist. Which might land me on suicide watch. I had no desire to make a bad situation worse.

Only one good thought came to me. At least I didn't have any pets to worry about. A few months ago, I'd found a cat in my stairwell and taken her in. She'd had two kittens. I'd enjoyed the company, but decided my situation was too risky to keep them myself. If I got locked up, like I was now, they'd starve to death if no one went to get them. Kelly's school age kids, Brianna and Chris, had been begging for a pet, and she took the whole little family in.

I wondered how the cats were doing with Kelly in the hospital. Kelly shouldn't be gone that long, and if the bikers just left them alone, they should be okay.

And the kids. How were they dealing with this whole thing? Had to be tough on them. I needed to think about something else. I tried to size up my cellmate.

He didn't show any reaction at all, just stared at the wall and ignored me. I held out my hand to the kid. He was tall and lanky, his shoulders hunched dejectedly. "Jesse," I said.

He turned away from me.

Shrugging, I said, "Suit yourself."

"You just better leave me alone," he said, his voice harsh. "I didn't get picked up on no stupid possession charges like most of the guys in here. I'm looking at *assault* charges."

Tough guy wannabe, I thought. He was right about most of the inmates in the jail being held on CDS—controlled dangerous substance, mostly narcotics—charges, but one thing about a county lockup is that often no one knows whether they were dealing with a kid who did something stupid or a true psychopath. We *were* in high security housing, and they must have had a reason for putting him here. CDS charges alone wouldn't justify that.

"How about you?" he asked.

I turned to eye him. Hard to see much in the dark. "Right now, parole violation."

"Parole violation." He spit out the words, contempt in his voice. "What, they catch you using again? Dirty piss or something? How much backup time you got?"

I considered how much I wanted to tell him, but decided there was no point not telling him the truth. "Maybe another twenty years or so. Depend on how much good time I could pick up."

I heard the sharp intake of his breath. "That don't sound like usual drug charges," he said. "What did they get you for?"

"Couple of things. Pretty much all related."

"Like what?"

No point in lying now. "Conspiracy. Possession of a handgun during commission of a felony. Murder."

He made a strangled sound, kicked off his shoes and lay down, curling into a ball and away from the wall, his eyes open wide and staring.

I don't think he slept well the rest of that night.

* * * *

"Breakfast!"

Dressed only in jail-issued shorts and a T-shirt, I slid down from the top bunk and slipped my feet into the shower shoes. An inmate in kitchen whites stood by the hatch in the cell door, a tray in each hand.

The CO stood behind him, watching.

I took one tray and set it on the steel shelf set into the cinderblocks against the back of the cell.

Glancing at my cell buddy, still lying in the bottom bunk facing the wall, his blanket pulled up over his shoulders. I asked, "Ain't you gonna eat?"

No response.

"Don't you want your breakfast?"

He didn't look up at me. "Shut up." Even less friendly than last night.

I shrugged and turned to the kitchen worker. "Can I take it for him? He might change his mind."

"No skin off my teeth," he said, slipping the other tray through the hatch. I put it next to the other one.

The actively circulating air was damp and chilly. The cell had no window. I peered through the grilled door into the brightly lit common area, which at this security level wouldn't be used much. No windows there that I could see. No skylight, either. *This was going to be depressing. As if being locked up wasn't depressing enough.*

The oversized orange jumpsuit I'd been given the night before was at the foot of my bunk and I reached for it, pulled it on, and snapped it.

Not very warm, but a bit better than just the underwear. I could do with some socks and a sweatshirt, but the prospects of getting them didn't look very good. Neither did the possibility of a shave. I rubbed my cheek. Maybe I should just grow a beard.

Breakfast wasn't bad. A good-sized square of reconstituted dried eggs, two pieces of toast which actually had a smear of margarine on them, a carton of juice, and one of milk. I had no idea how quickly someone would be around to collect the trays again, so I scarfed mine down.

My cell buddy didn't stir. I looked longingly at his tray. "You gonna eat that?" I asked him.

"Shut up," he said again.

This was going to be cheerful. First no natural light, now I was going to be locked in twenty three hours a day with somebody who wasn't saying anything but "shut up."

We were in the restricted, high security cellblock. People were assigned here because they were considered dangerous, escape risks, or crazy.

How about this guy? An assault charge didn't seem reason enough to be assigned here, but I didn't know the circumstances. I hoped he wasn't a total crazy, although he wasn't giving me any indication to the contrary.

"Look," I said. "I'm thinking we're gonna be locked in here together for a lot of time so we might as well make the best of it."

He didn't move, but he said, "I bet you're not gonna be here long. I'm not going anywhere soon." He choked on the words. I hoped he wasn't going to start crying. Can't say as I'd blame him, but I never knew what to do when anybody did that. Especially when I was locked in with them.

"If all they get me for is the violation and they decide to go ahead with it, I'll be on the Thursday night bus to the diagnostics center," I said. "Then on to wherever they're holding parole violators waiting for a hearing. But if I pick up new charges, they'll hold me here while they take care of them."

"You'll have a bail hearing and probably get sprung."

I laughed. "Hearing, maybe. That's standard procedure. Ain't no bail gonna get set. And even if they did set it, ain't nobody gonna come up with it."

Stirring slightly, he said, "Don't you know nobody who'll go your bail?"

"Nope. And if someone *did* come up with the ten percent, no bail bondsman in his right mind would take it."

He sat up but didn't look at me. "Didn't nobody go mine, either."

"At least you got it set. How much is it?"

"Five thousand."

"That means, even if a bail bondsman'll take it, somebody's got to come up with five hundred dollars. That's a fair amount."

"Really?"

"Yeah. And then they don't get back all of it, either. Bail bondsman keeps ten percent of that. Fifty dollars. You know somebody's got that kind of money just lying around and can afford to take the fifty dollar hit when it's returned? Especially on a weekend?"

He paused thoughtfully. "Not really."

"Besides, if you think you're gonna pick up some time anyhow, you might as well get a start on it."

"Huh?"

"Look, they always give you credit on your sentence for time served. And if you're only looking at a short bit—a year or so—and you been locked up for a while, the sentencing judge sometimes just says 'time served' and cuts you loose. That can be less time than if you'd been out on bail the whole time. And you're *done*."

"A whole year? That's not a short bit."

I laughed again. "Well, it's certainly not long. You wouldn't even get sent up state for that, just serve it here in the county lockup."

"Up state?"

"You know. Prison."

He shivered. "Prison."

Was he going to start repeating everything I said?

He shook his head. "I hadn't thought of it like that. Just that my mom was letting me rot in here."

"You got a ways to go before you rot. Meanwhile, you want your breakfast?"

"Nah. You can have it."

I took his tray. "You got to eat *sometime*," I said. But maybe not right now. I stuffed his eggs and toast into my mouth and downed his juice and milk before he could change his mind. "Thanks."

He threw his blanket back and eased off his bunk, stepping up to the all-in-one steel plumbing fixture. Although he was bigger than me, he really was just a kid, and he'd slept in his jumpsuit.

Sitting on the edge of his bunk, he raked his hair forward over his face with his fingers but I could see he was all bruised up and swollen.

"What the hell happened to you?" I asked.

"Got in a fight," he said.

"Here in the jail?"

"Yeah."

That explained why he was in K-pod. "How'd the other guy make out?"

He took a deep breath. "*Three* other guys. I don't know what happened to them."

"You give as good as you get on the fight?"

"Huh?"

I sighed. "This the first time you been locked up?"

"Yeah." He sat up a little straighter.

"Well, sometimes you got to fight. Usually it don't do no good. So I try to mostly keep out of it. But if you *do* get caught up in a scrape, make sure you give a good account of yourself and do some damage. Then people will think twice about starting with you next time."

He looked confused. "The guards broke it up. Pepper spray. That stuff really burns."

I nodded. "Good to know. Some places, they just let you fight it out and write up the reports afterwards. And send you for medical attention if you need it."

Looking at my face, he said, "What happened to *you*? A fight?"

"Nah. I got a little upset when the cops were questioning me, so they got a little rough."

"A *cop* did that to you?"

"Yeah. Slammed me down on the hood of his car."

"What did you do to him?"

"Nothing, really. Just moved too fast and made him nervous."

"You pick up resisting arrest charges?"

"Not that I know of, but they could always file them if they wanted to."

He leaned forward and stared at the floor between his feet. "What's gonna happen to me now?"

I shrugged. "Depends. You know the person you assaulted? Or was it just some random victim?"

"Why would I go after somebody random?" he asked. "It was my mother's boyfriend."

"And why would you go after your mother's boyfriend? Was he hitting her or something?"

He set his mouth stubbornly. "He was saying nasty things to her. Don't nobody can say nasty things to *my* mother and get away with it."

"Your mother can't take care of herself?" I asked. "And there ain't *no* legal basis for a physical response to a verbal provocation. She happy you stepped in?"

He raised his eyebrows. "What?"

"Your mom. She like it that you butted in between her and her boy-friend?"

"I don't think so." He frowned.

"So why should she bail you out? Even if she could find the money? So you could come back and beat up on her boyfriend some more?"

"She's my *mother*."

"So?"

"Well…" He scratched his chin and looked at me. "Would *you* let somebody call your mother a fucking whore?"

I shook my head. "My mother died when I was a little kid. An acci-dent where she worked. I don't remember her. For all I know, she might have been a fucking whore."

"Who'd you live with? Grandparents? Your dad?"

"Never had any grandparents I ever knew about. And my dad was locked up most of the time until I was in my teens. Foster homes, mostly."

He shifted on the bunk. The flame resistant plastic covering on the mattress crinkled. Looking up at me, he held out his hand. "Willis here. Sorry I was such an SOB."

I took his hand and shook it. Better to be on good terms with a cell buddy. We'd likely spend hours and hours together.

"Did you do it?" he asked.

"Did I do what?"

"Murder somebody?"

My turn to shift uncomfortably. "Well, I was convicted of it."

"Yeah. But did you *do* it?"

I never knew how to answer questions like that. Shrugging, I said, "I won't argue with the fact that I'm guilty."

"You actually killed somebody?"

"It's not that simple." I pulled on the shoulder of the oversized jump-suit, trying to get it to lie comfortably. "In this state, if you're involved in a felony that results in a death, you're guilty of murder."

"So that's what happened? Somebody died?"

"Yeah. A drug dealer. One of my older brothers probably shot him. I was the lookout outside. I didn't know anybody'd been shot until it was too late."

"What'd you mean, too late?"

"I was a kid. Sixteen. Both my brothers were over eighteen, with pretty impressive rap sheets already. We agreed that if anything went wrong, I'd take the blame. Worst I thought I'd get was six months in boot camp. Or a year and a half in juvie hall."

"If you were sixteen, can't they hold you until you're twenty one?"

"Yeah, if the charges are serious enough. But it gets worse than that. Murder charges go to adult court if you're fourteen or older. I didn't know that. And I didn't know somebody was dead. So I didn't deny it when the cops asked if I was in the apartment. Big mistake."

"Did they think you were the triggerman?"

"Yeah. My public defender told me I'd better cop a plea or I'd get life. So I did."

Willis fell silent. I didn't feel much like talking, either. We sat, both looking at the tiny cracks in the concrete floor.

One newspaper got delivered to the cellblock, but the CO was sitting at a desk in the dayroom reading it. The single TV droned on with a Sunday morning religious service. We couldn't see it very well from our cell.

"You got anything to read?" I asked Willis hopefully.

He shook his head. "I don't read much," he said.

"You stay locked up long, you will," I told him. "You know if they got some kind of library service here?"

"I dunno."

If he came over here, I'd ask the CO. He might be able to get me a book. I wouldn't be fussy about what kind.

Looked like this was going to be a long day.

I lay back on my bunk and tried to think of anything but Kelly. Not easy. I remembered what I'd been reading back at my apartment. It was a nonfiction account of the Battle of Antietam during the Civil War.

Probably not gonna get a chance to finish it. If I stayed locked up, the landlord would clean out the apartment when my rent ran out. Get a new tenant. Would he bother to return the book to the library?

At least the cat and her kittens were at Kelly's place.

I'd lose my job. Never get a job as good as that one again. Not that I'd ever be likely to need it if I picked up new charges. I'd be working in the prison laundry again. For the princely inmate pay of a dollar a day and the chance to get out of my cell.

At work, they'd have to pull in a substitute forklift driver from another shift until they could train a new one. Only two lift drivers on our shift, me and Kelly.

Kelly. My breath caught and I coughed. Tears gathered in my eyes. *Damn. I wasn't going to start bawling now, was I?* I rolled over to face the wall and swallowed the sob that rose in my throat. *What was going on with her?* I half-dozed, trying to think about something else. Anything else.

"Jesse?" Willis said.

"Yeah?" Thank goodness, no trace of tears in my voice.

"Can I ask you a question?"

"I don't got too many answers, but ask away."

"You know those guys I said I was in a fight with?"

"No, I don't know them, but I know what you're talking about."

"I kind of got involved in some shit. Out on the street. And they think I might have snitched on them and their buddies."

"Did you?"

"Hell, no. So far I don't think the cops know I was involved. And I hope it stays that way."

"What kind of shit was it?"

He hesitated.

"You don't got to tell me if you don't want to."

"I got to tell *somebody*." His eye twitched.

"Well, no, you really don't. But I'm not gonna snitch."

"These guys, they been boosting cars."

"You been boosting them, too?"

"No. I just been locating them."

"Locating? What do you mean?"

"Going around and finding cars like they got on their list. Mostly late-model luxury types. When I find one, I call this number and give its location. They give me ten bucks for each one I call in. And fifty if it works out."

"If what works out?"

He looked at me like I was dense. "If they boost it."

"That's not much money for the risks you been taking."

"Not much risk. I don't *do* nothing but call this number. And they gave me a cell phone."

"You ever heard of conspiracy charges?"

"I've *heard* of them. But I'm not real sure what they are."

"They're when you're part of a criminal operation but don't necessarily do much. Like calling in the location of a car that's then stolen. You have any idea what the penalties for conspiracy are?"

"No."

"Same as for whatever crime they're conspiracy to. In this case, grand theft auto. Or even carjacking."

He sat for a minute, not saying anything.

"And you get involved with some pretty nasty characters. Who'll beat you up as soon as look at you," I added.

"Yeah. I think I got that part figured out. But it's easy money. And most of them are making a lot more than I did. It's a profitable scheme."

"Are those the guys who beat you up?"

"Well, that's some of them."

"Look where the 'profitable scheme' got them. Locked up."

We heard the door from the hallway into the cellblock slide open. Boot steps echoed as a CO strode down the row of cells. I could hear the faint jangle of his keys. I lay there, waiting for him to pass by. He stopped at our door.

"Jesse Damon?"

Shaking my head to clear the cobwebs, I scrambled down from the bunk and went to the door. A CO stood there, papers in one hand and his radio in the other.

"Yes, sir?" I said.

"Pop the door on K-14," he said into the radio.

The door slid open. I stood there waiting to be told what to do.

"Someone to see you."

I stepped out of the cell. The door closed behind me. Willis sat on his bunk and stared at us. "Visitor?" he asked.

"Not likely," I said. "Especially on a Sunday morning."

"You got your ID?" the CO asked.

I showed him the plastic bracelet on my wrist. He tried to tug it off, but it didn't come. Frowning, he lifted my hand and read the information, checking it against the paper, and looked at the tiny photograph then up at my face. He glanced at Willis. "You both so beat up, it's hard to tell who's who."

He stepped back and let me precede him out to the door from the housing unit to the hallway, where he radioed a request to have it opened. Then he gestured down the hallway toward the front of the jail.

I shuffled on ahead of him, trying to keep the shower shoes from falling off and the legs of the jumpsuit from trailing on the floor. We got to a door again—was it the same attorney visitation room I'd been in last night?—and he radioed for that to be opened.

It was the same room. And Montgomery was inside, this time dressed in a grey pinstripe suit with a pale pink shirt and a striped tie. He shook his head when he saw me.

"You look rough. Not bad enough your face is all bruised up. You could fit another inmate or two in that jumpsuit with you and still be able to snap it."

I grinned. "Yeah. I guess they don't want to worry that the jumpsuits are gonna be too small for anybody they get in after the laundry room's shut at night."

"Well, by the size of that thing, I think they've got that covered." He sat on the edge of the table. "A few things I want you to tell me."

I felt my stomach churn. "About Kelly?"

"Yeah. And about the people she hangs with."

"I don't know who she hangs with. Apart from me. And that hasn't been much lately."

He raised his chiseled eyebrows on his dark forehead. "I'm trying to figure out what happened to your girlfriend here. I'd think the least you could do was cooperate."

"If I know anything that'll help you find out who raped her, I'll tell you. But I don't know all that much."

"She seeing anyone besides you?"

I shrugged. "Not that she told me. But I never asked."

"Why is that?"

"None of my business, really. She made it pretty clear she didn't want a tight relationship. At least not with me."

"How did she make that clear?"

"She *said* so. 'Don't expect this to be exclusive' or something."

He suppressed a smile. "And how did you feel about that?"

I tried to keep the hitch out of my voice. "I had to accept that. I mean, what have I got going for me that I could ask her for any kind of exclusive relationship?"

"So if she was seeing someone else and not telling you, you'd be okay with that?"

Shifting from one foot to the other, I said, "Well, not exactly *okay* with it. But it was one of those 'my way or the highway' things with her, and I took what I could get."

"You settled for the crumbs, huh?"

"I guess. If you want to look at it like that."

"How did *you* look at it?"

Without thinking, I blurted out, "She was the best thing that ever happened to me."

He cocked his head. "Sex that good?"

I looked away from him. "It's not just the sex. That's a big part of it, sure. I mean, I been locked up for years. But it was the way she *treated* me."

"Like how?"

"Like a regular *person*. Not like a convict on parole. We fixed dinner for her kids. Watched TV sometimes. Just spent time together. It's hard to explain."

He looked thoughtful. "I think I get it. But tell me, was she seeing any of the Predators that you know of?"

"She said they were hanging around her dad a lot. So of course she was *seeing* them. But you mean like sleeping with any of them?"

"Yeah."

"Well, they're bikers. They're not real fussy about who they jump into bed with. But I don't think Kelly would go for that."

Montgomery narrowed his eyes. "But you haven't known her for that long. You don't know for sure."

My jaw tightened, and I wanted to argue with him. I knew, though, that wouldn't do any good. And he was right about me not knowing her for that long. I took a deep breath, unclenched my teeth and said, "I guess."

"She didn't say anything about one in particular?"

"Not to me."

"Or about any of their women getting jealous?"

"Probably wouldn't bother the women if they screwed her, or anybody else. Happens all the time. Only way one of the women would get upset was if her man asked her for his colors back so he could give them to someone else."

"That happen with Kelly that you know of?"

"Look, I been steering clear of Kelly's place since her dad came to stay there. It was almost like a second clubhouse for the Predators. I don't know why they decided it was a better place to hang out, but they did. I could get myself in a lot of trouble just being there."

"So maybe Kelly was getting lonesome? Or horny?"

My throat began to close up. Not a train of thought I wanted to pursue. "She sure wasn't getting any from *me* lately."

"And she likes her sex, doesn't she?"

I had to admit that was true. "Yeah."

"Maybe she was getting tight with one of them?"

"It don't sound like her, but I guess it could happen." Montgomery stood up. "I've got some good news for you."

"Is that so? I could use some good news."

"Kelly's come around some. Gonna spend another day or two in the hospital, maybe go on to rehab for her shoulder, but she's awake. Says she'd had a few drinks and don't remember everything, but she's sure it wasn't you who raped her."

I breathed a sigh of relief. On a couple of counts.

"She says you weren't even there."

"Is she gonna be okay?"

"I think so. A bit battered up, but nothing permanent. At least physically."

"Did she say who did it?"

"Yep. One of her daddy's acquaintances."

"Who?"

He clasped his hands in front of him. The green jewel in his ring glistened in the overhead light. "You really think *I'm* gonna tell you? So you can figure out how to get the crap beat out of him?"

I shook my head. "I'll probably find out anyhow. And I don't think I'll be beating the crap out of anybody."

"I wouldn't expect you to do it yourself. But I wouldn't put it past you to make sure it happened. Or worse."

"Or worse?"

"Yeah. I know how you guys think. Something like making sure his dick got a whole lot shorter. I'm not going to be the one responsible for that kind of mutilation, even if the guy deserves it. We've got an APB for him. With any luck, we'll pick him up before Old Buckles and some of his biker buddies find him. Or you."

No point in trying to tell him I wouldn't be out for revenge. I said, "So what does that mean for me now?"

"That means they cut you loose."

I could hardly believe it. "You got in touch with my PO? On a weekend? And he's okay with that?"

Montgomery looked at me. "You know Ramirez."

I did. I counted myself lucky to have Mr. Ramirez as my parole officer. He took his job seriously. He was of the opinion that if I was going to abscond, I'd have done so. A while ago. And he was right.

He felt the best place for any offender who could handle it was out on parole, holding down a job, and paying taxes, not being a burden on society.

I'd have to figure out some way to say thanks to Mr. Ramirez at my next parole appointment.

"And one more thing, Jesse," Montgomery said.

"Yeah?"

"If I were you, I'd stay away from Kelly for the time being."

"You said she's still in the hospital?"

"Yes."

I nodded, but that was one piece of advice I wasn't going to be following.

He moved over to the door and called for the CO.

CHAPTER 4

A few hours later, I walked out the front door of the jail into the gathering darkness. I was wearing my own clothes which were beginning to feel pretty grungy. I had my wallet and apartment key back in my pocket. My hair tie had gone missing, but I wasn't going to complain about anything minor that might delay my release. I brushed back my straggly brown hair and tried to tuck it into my collar so it would stay out of my face. And I still needed a shave.

Willis had been right about me getting sprung after all.

The hospital was only a few blocks away and, despite Montgomery's warning, it was the first place I headed.

The building was in the center of a well-lit parking lot. I approached the emergency room entrance, and I walked up to it. There were a few ambulances and a patrol car pulled up by the door. A cop stood on the sidewalk, talking into his radio. Not a good place for me to be, so I kept going around the side of the building.

Kelly might have been brought in that way, but by now she'd be somewhere else. I hoped not in intensive care or another place where they had visitors limited to immediate family and kept track of them.

I circled around to the front of the building, stopping by a huge lighted sign by the end of the circular driveway. "Rothsburg Memorial Hospital," it announced, and listed a series of destinations with arrows pointing in different directions.

As I tried to figure out where I needed to go, a couple of chopped Harleys pulled up to the front door, each with a passenger behind the rider. One was a customized trike. Stepping back into the shadow of the sign, I watched as two women climbed off the rear seats. The backs of their leather jackets sported club colors, but I wasn't near enough to read them. They tugged at their hair and clothes, straightening themselves out before they headed inside.

I'd take bets they had come to see Kelly.

The bikes slid around the driveway and eased to a stop near where I stood. One rider, a tall weedy guy with a bandana tied over his hair, knocked the kickstand into place and dismounted. The beefy trike rider, his waist-length grey hair and full beard in braids, straddled his seat.

I knew I'd seen that trike before, in Kelly's garage, where she kept it for her dad while he was in prison. I took another look at the rider as he took off his WWI-style helmet and glanced in my direction.

Old Buckles, Kelly's dad. Wasn't he going to go in to see her?

"Jesse?" he asked.

We didn't really know each other, but we'd been locked up in the same prison for years, both in medium security cellblocks. He'd been in and out, doing life on the installment plan, while I'd been a more or less permanent resident. He'd spent a lot of time working as a prison commissary clerk. The temptations to someone working that job were everywhere, so any inmate who they kept working in that position had to have a certain amount of integrity. And I'd heard he wasn't above sneaking something extra, like a few stamps or a bottle of aspirin, into somebody's order if he knew they were having a hard time and needed it.

I stepped forward. "Yeah. You gonna go to see Kelly?"

He leaned back and pulled out a Roll-Rite, passing it under his nose. I couldn't tell whether it was tobacco or weed. Or a mixture. "Maybe later. I hate hospitals. The ladies gonna check things out for us." He belched and pulled out a lighter.

The other guy stepped up to me, his fists clenched. "You Jesse? Kelly supposed to be your old lady?" he asked between clenched teeth.

I looked him over. I couldn't see the backs of their leather jackets from this angle, but I had no doubt both he and Old Buckles showed club colors, just like the women. A leering skull of a saber tooth tiger with "Predators" embroidered above and street names below.

Bikers had their own ideas about how a relationship was supposed to operate between a woman and her man. They weren't exactly mainstream ideas, but they seemed to work all right for them.

They'd never work for me and Kelly, though.

"Kelly's her own woman," I said. "She don't belong to me or nobody else."

He ignored that. "A man's supposed to take care of his woman. Not let her get beat up."

Who was this guy? I would have understood if Old Buckles was bent out of shape. Kelly was his kid. But this guy?

He wasn't backing down. Looked like I'd have to handle this whether I wanted to or not. "What's it to you?" I asked, locking my gaze on his.

Old Buckles took a pull on his smoke and said, "Hey, Funk…"

The guy raised his fist and took a swing at me.

Since I'd been looking toward Old Buckles, I didn't dodge quite fast enough, and the punch caught me in the face. My already battered nose spurted blood. Again.

Reacting without thinking, I slammed my right fist into his gut, then caught him in the face with a left uppercut when he hunched over, and followed it up with a knee to the groin. He fell to the ground in a ball, moaning and clasping his privates with both hands.

I started to raise my boot above his head when my brain started working again. In prison, the penalty for fighting would be a month in disciplinary segregation. Here, if it came to the attention of the authorities, it would be street charges. A one-way ticket back to prison.

And if I seriously injured this guy, it would certainly come to the attention of the authorities. We were right outside a hospital, for the love of Hades. No better place for an injured person to come to the attention of the authorities.

Reluctantly, I lowered my foot and backed up a few steps.

Old Buckles hadn't moved. He looked at the guy on the sidewalk and shook his head. "I was gonna tell Funky Joe to lay off and leave you alone, but looks like you took care of it, huh?"

I shrugged.

"You gonna go see Kelly?" he asked.

"I was hoping to. Or at least find out how she's doing." I wiped my nose with the sleeve of my jacket. Not a smart move. How was I ever going to get all that blood out of the wool?

He gestured toward the door. "Go ahead. Joe here'll be okay. I'll keep an eye on him. We don't want no trouble. Not with the cops or nobody else."

"Thanks." I rubbed my skinned knuckles.

"Don't be thanking me too soon," he warned me. "I haven't figured out what happened to my little girl yet, so I don't know whose fault this is. But somebody's gonna pay. And you're definitely not off the list of possibilities."

I nodded. It was hard to think of the substantial Kelly as anybody's little girl, but he *was* her daddy.

"And go clean yourself up before you go see her," he said. "You'd scare the devil himself looking like that." He took another drag. A faint sweet scent mingled with the tobacco.

I had to grin at the idea of me scaring the devil.

As soon as I got through the front door of the hospital, I looked around for a restroom. My face had been pretty battered in the last few days and was undoubtedly still bruising up. I could feel the sticky blood all over my mouth and chin, and dripping down my neck.

A gift shop was right near the entrance. Next to it was a big men's room. I ducked in. In addition to the urinal, it had two stalls, one a large handicapped stall with a deep sink at wheelchair height. I went in that one and latched the door behind me.

Using paper towels and some liquid soap that stung the raw spots, I scrubbed my face. Not too bad, I thought as I peered into the mirror. I wadded up pieces of paper towel and stuffed them up my nostrils, hoping to stop the bleeding. My nose was a bit misshapen, but not too swollen. My jaw was bruised and dark, but I hadn't shaved in a few days, and the five o'clock shadow helped hide it.

My hair, though, was a tangled, matted mess. Money was always tight ,and as long as I could keep my hair tucked out of the way under my hard hat at work, nobody cared how long it was, so I'd been postponing getting a haircut.

Sticky clumps of hair hung by either side of my face. I tried pulling them apart, but it was obvious I'd have to wash the blood out.

I took off my jacket and shirt, laying them over a grab bar. Then I lathered my hands with a lot of the soap and bent into the sink, rubbing the suds into my hair and rinsing. It was awkward, but it worked.

The door to the hallway opened. I froze. Water dripped from my hair onto my shoulders as I backed up so that if anyone looked under the door, my feet appeared to be near the toilet. I tried to convince myself that no one would bother to check. Why would they? But I held my breath as I heard the newcomer splash into the urinal, then the flush of water. He left.

He hadn't washed his hands. I hoped he wasn't a hospital employee.

I took my jacket and rinsed the blood out of the sleeve as well as I could. It was an old hunter's jacket I'd gotten at Goodwill, a black and red buffalo check, so at least the stain wasn't all that noticeable. The jacket itself, however, stood out like a sore thumb. I folded it so the quilted black lining showed instead of the garish plaid.

Easing the wads of paper towel out of my nose, I didn't breathe for a few seconds while I waited to see if blood would start dripping again.

It didn't.

I tried to breathe through my mouth.

Putting on my shirt and tucking my wet hair behind my ears, I studied my reflection in the mirror again. Not perfect, but I didn't look like quite such a deranged madman as I had before.

Now to figure out how to get up to see Kelly. Without being noticed so that if—or more likely when—Montgomery started asking questions, people wouldn't remember me. That eliminated going up to the front desk and asking for her room number.

The large waiting room was almost deserted except for a line of people waiting to talk to a single, harried lady who was manning the information desk.

Hallways led off in several directions and an alcove with a bank of elevators sat in one corner.

Partially shielded by a plant with big leaves, I sat down in a plastic chair by the elevator bank and watched people hurry by. Joining them and just wandering the hallways without having any idea of where Kelly was didn't seem like such a good idea.

I was in luck. The two biker chicks came from a hallway carrying huge paper cups and a take-out bag. Their boot heels clicking on the tile floor, they strode purposefully toward the elevators.

People moved aside and let them by. Their boots, tight jeans, and leather vests were crisscrossed with chains. As I expected, they had embroidered patches on the back of their jackets with saber tooth tiger skulls, "Predators" above and the women's names, Li'l Mama and Black Rose, below. Beneath that, Black Rose's said, "Property of Razorback" and Li'l Mama's said, "Property of Funky Joe."

Funky Joe was the guy I'd left lying on the sidewalk outside.

I got to my feet and followed them, figuring they were on their way to Kelly's room. When the next elevator came, they got in, and no one else got in with them, although several people had been waiting longer than they had. I watched the numbers over the elevator door. It stopped on the third floor.

The fewer people who noticed me, the better.

A whole bunch of people got onto the next elevator. I entered with them and got off with a small knot when we reached the third floor. I tried to step out quickly, hoping to catch a glimpse of Black Rose or Li'l Mama, but got caught behind a hefty woman with a big shopping bag, and by the time I got out in the hallway, they were nowhere in sight.

Most of the other people crowded around the nursing station, asking for room numbers and updates. I wasn't about to go do that and give them a chance to remember me, so I glanced around.

The hallway ended abruptly a few hundred feet in one direction but stretched a long way in the other. Deciding to play the odds, I set off down the long portion, glancing in each room as I passed, looking to see if something would tell me which room was Kelly's.

My luck held. I heard the clink of chains and sharp boot steps on the polished floor as I passed room 307. An elderly lady lay in the bed nearest the door, her eyes shut, but I could see Li'l Mama's tight blue-jeaned derriere disappear behind the fabric curtain that separated the two beds.

The trick to sneaking in anywhere, I knew, was to act like being there was no big deal. Which in this case meant continuing confidently past the room while I considered what to do.

At the end of the hallway was a kind of lounge with a few people sitting there, some in wheelchairs. I turned around and headed back toward room 307. This time, I slipped into the room and pulled up a chair between the head of the old woman's bed and the curtain, trusting the position and the subdued light to shield me from Kelly and her visitors.

The lights on this side of the room were dimmed. A gentle wheezing came from some kind of machine that had a tube leading to the patient's nostrils. The person lying on the bed was an old, old woman, her head barely making a dent on the pillow, her eyes closed. Thank goodness she didn't have any visitors. Until me.

I turned my head toward the woman in the bed so my face could not be seen from the doorway and listened to the conversation beyond the curtain.

One of the women was talking. That high pitched voice *had* to belong to Li'l Mama. "Your dad was thinking about coming up, but he decided to wait until you feel better. Or maybe get discharged. He hates hospitals. And he's fit to be tied."

Someone—Kelly?—murmured something, but I couldn't make out the words. I leaned forward, straining to hear.

The old woman stirred. "Are you there?" she said in a voice that was barely a whisper. Her parchment hand moved on the sheet, reaching toward me but moving only an inch or so.

"Are you there?" she asked more urgently.

Feeling like a total fraud but not wanting her to make a fuss, I put my work-roughened hand over her fragile one. "I'm here," I whispered.

Her clawlike hand grasped mine with surprising strength. "Otto!" she said. "You came at last. Just sit with me for a while. It's been such a long time."

I had no idea who Otto was, but I wasn't about to correct her. I patted her hand with my other one and said, "I'm right here."

"Thank God. I don't want to die alone."

Die? I looked at her in alarm. She *did* look like she could die any minute. Where her wispy, white hair was brushed aside I could see the pink skin on her scalp. Her ears were sunk back against her head, and the earlobes were shriveled. Her eyelids looked translucent, but she didn't open her eyes. Which was just as well, because if she looked, she might see I wasn't Otto.

Please don't die while I'm here, I thought. I wouldn't have any idea what to do.

"I'm so tired," she said.

"Rest," I told her.

"Don't leave me."

I might not be Otto, but I could stay for a little while if it comforted her. "I'm right here."

A slight smile played on her lips, and her grip on my hand relaxed, retaining only a slight hold. I sat there and listened to what I could catch of the conversation on the other side of the curtain.

"Your dad says he's gonna get them taken care of," Black Rose was saying in her deep voice. "If he catches up with them before the cops do, they're gonna *wish* they got locked up."

Again the murmuring that I couldn't make out.

"Nobody's sure yet," Li'l Mama said. "But your dad wants to know everyone who was involved. It's too late now to keep it in the club. Once an ambulance got called and it was obvious you had to get to the hospital, there's no way it can be quiet. The cops have the report from the emergency room. They're gonna get the results from the rape kit, so there won't be any doubt."

Black Rose spoke up. "Some of the guys are trying to talk your dad into letting the cops handle it. He's still on parole, and if they find out he's out to make somebody pay, he'll be violated. Better he should let someone else take care of it."

They stopped talking. I wished they'd say more.

The old lady's breathing became shallower and more regular. Her mouth drooped open, and a bubble formed at the corner.

A nurse hurried in, her footsteps hushed by the thick soles of her pristine white duty shoes. I kept turned toward the lady in the bed, hoping the nurse wouldn't notice the bruises on my face too much. Or be able to describe me if Montgomery came asking questions. I was glad I'd thought to have my distinctive jacket folded up next to me instead of wearing it.

"I'm so glad you came," the nurse said in a soothing voice. "She was so hoping you would. The social worker has been trying to contact family. We were beginning to think she had no one left. Are you Otto, the son?"

My gut twisted inside me. How could I lie about this? But how could I not? I said, "Yeah." The words choked in my throat.

"It's all right if you cry," she said, mistaking the reason for my husky voice. "Losing a loved one is always hard, even if she has lived a good and rich life. But it means a lot to her to have you here. She's calmer than she's been since she arrived."

"How much longer do you think she has?"

"Who knows? You could talk to the doctor when he comes around next. You do know we have a 'Do not resuscitate' order, don't you?"

I didn't, but I nodded. Sounded like a good idea to me. "Will she wake up again?" I asked, uncomfortable with the idea that her Otto would be gone when she did. Even if he was a fraud.

"Maybe. Maybe not. I think there's a chaplain on tonight. Shall I send him up?"

The lady seemed to grow thinner, and her skin more transparent as I watched. "Yes, please."

The nurse nodded and drew the curtain around the foot of the bed. Then she went over to the other side of the room.

"Time to check vital signs," she said, her voice no longer hushed and somber.

I heard restless movements from beyond the curtain. "We gotta be going anyhow," Black Rose said.

"Hey, Kelly, somebody'll be by to see how you're doing tomorrow. I'll tell your dad it's okay to come up. You want to talk to him, right?"

The answer was too soft for me to hear.

"Will someone from the sexual assault crisis team be checking on her again?" Li'l Mama asked.

The answer was too hushed for me to catch.

I listened as the leather heels from the women's biker boots clicked past and went into the hallway. My nose caught a whiff of leather, oil, and cigarettes as they passed by.

The nurse talked cheerfully to Kelly as she worked. "Try to get some sleep. The doctor doesn't want to give you another sleeping pill—you had such a bad reaction last time. If you can get some rest, you'll probably feel better in the morning. You need to begin the healing process."

A chair was set down on the floor with a thud. A drawer squeaked open and then shut. The lights dimmed and the nurse hurried out of the room, not stopping to peek in on us on the other side of the room.

The old lady's hand slipped from mine. Her breathing was slow but regular. Then the next breath didn't come. A smile still played on her lips. She seemed to shrink into the bedding. When I carefully withdrew my hand from hers, she didn't move. I smoothed the sheet that covered her.

Trying not to disturb her—although if I was right she might be beyond being disturbed—I got to my feet and slid around the curtain to the other side of the room. Kelly lay there, her face swollen and her eyes shut. Was she asleep already?

"Kelly?" I said.

Her eyes flickered open and took a moment to focus on me. "You!" she said.

I grinned and reached for her hand. "Yeah. Me. How're you doing?"

She pulled her hand back and tucked it under the covers. "I've been better. You come to apologize?"

That threw me. Apologize? I wasn't sure what she meant, but right now it didn't matter. "If you want me to," I said.

"And you think that's going to make things all better?"

This conversation wasn't going anything like I'd expected. "What do you mean?"

She started to sit up, winced, and lay back down again. "You really think you can do this to me and come in and apologize and everything's gonna be all right again?"

"What?"

"My dad'll be looking for you and whoever else was part of this. You just better hope you get locked up before he finds you."

CHAPTER 5

My head spinning with questions I had no way to answer, I hurried out of room, barely glancing at the old woman, whose motionless form seemed definitely smaller than before.

I didn't want to run into anyone, especially any of the bikers. I dashed down the stairs instead of taking the elevator and found a door marked "Emergency Exit Only. Alarm Will Sound."

The hell with the alarm. As far as I was concerned, this *was* an emergency.

I shoved the door open and left the hospital.

The alarm sounded. Loudly.

The door slammed behind me. I was in a parking lot on the side of the hospital. Breaking into a run would only draw more unwanted attention, so I suppressed the urge and walked quickly through the parking lot, crossed the street, and plunged into dark alley between two tall buildings. I pressed myself up against the wall.

Stupid thing for me to do, set off an alarm.

Trying to keep in the shadows, I peered out of the alley back toward the emergency exit door. The alarm continued to shrill.

An elderly security guard, his radio grasped firmly in his hand, approached the door from the outside. No urgency showed in his step. He looked around the parking lot, then took out a big key and unlocked the door. He stepped inside, letting it shut behind him. A few seconds later, he came out again and pushed the door closed, tugging on it to make sure it wouldn't open from the outside. He lifted the radio to his mouth, but I was too far away to hear what he said. The alarm quieted. Then he strolled back in the direction from which he had come.

I leaned back against the dirty brick wall of the alley and tried to think. What made Kelly blame me for the attack? She had to realize I wasn't *there*. Did she have a head injury that was messing with her mind? Some kind of traumatic brain injury?

Or was *I* the one with the problem? That was a scary thought. I couldn't have had some kind of blackout and done something horrible that I didn't remember, could I? I didn't use drugs or alcohol so it couldn't be a blackout caused by either of them. *Was I losing my mind?*

Montgomery had cut me loose. He'd based that on *something*. I had no idea how long it would take for DNA tests to come back from the forensics lab, but a few hours on a weekend seemed much too fast. Hadn't he said Kelly had told them the attacker *wasn't* me?

The throaty roar of accelerating motorcycles reached me, and two bikes swept around the corner and past me, their headlights glaring off the damp asphalt. I couldn't make out much as they passed the alley entrance, but I could see one was Old Buckles' trike. The women were on the backs, Li'l Mama behind Funky Joe and Black Rose with Old Buckles. I choked on the exhaust fumes. Or was it grief?

Was Kelly invoking the old outlaw biker rule of never involving the authorities if it could be avoided? The Predators stuck together, and they tended to take care of their own problems. Usually violently. A light rain began to fall. The road would be slippery. Glad I wasn't on two wheels. Or even three, exposed to the weather like that. Hitching up the collar of my jacket, I stepped out of the alley and headed for home. If Kelly didn't want to talk to me, I didn't see any way to find out why she thought I was involved in the attack. *Who could I talk to?*

Or, since Montgomery seemed satisfied that I wasn't involved, maybe I should just leave well enough alone.

And hope the bikers would, too. Fat chance.

The rain was beginning to freeze as it hit the ground. The stairs down from the sidewalk to my one-room apartment were getting slick. It might be Saturday night, but it would be a good night for me to spend at home.

I rummaged around in my single kitchen cupboard and the under-the-counter half refrigerator, looking for something to fix for supper. The last time I'd eaten had been breakfast at the jail. I'd missed lunch and been released before they served supper. *Lucky me.*

My food budget was limited, and it seemed like every time I went to the store, my staples of ramen noodles, peanut butter, eggs, and tuna went up in price. The jail's eggs had been edible, but I could fix better. I scrambled two eggs, slicing in part of an onion and green pepper. I hesitated before putting in an expensive slice of cheese, but decided to go for it. Then I toasted two pieces of cheap white bread and made myself a cup of instant coffee.

Making it all into a sandwich, I put it on my rickety table and sat in one of my two equally rickety chairs.

The only light came from a security light outside which overlooked the dumpster. My single window was placed high on the interior wall, but this was a basement apartment and the view was a knee-high one of the alley. Just enough light shone through it for me to eat by. It was quiet except for the lonesome sound of the rain, which sounded like it was changing to sleet.

Someday I was going to splurge on a radio, just for the long hours like this. Or even a TV. Right now I knew they were impossibly expensive luxuries.

The apartment was a single room, but it came furnished. Some people might find it less than satisfactory, with its decrepit, mismatched furniture, the kitchen and tiny bathroom stuck along one wall, and the lack of natural light. Those people hadn't spent years locked in a prison cell.

I reached over to the unsteady dresser and picked up a library book, flipping through the pages. The prison library had been my salvation for all those years I was locked up, and now the public library, free for anyone who could prove residency, was my main source of both entertainment and information. I would be eternally grateful to the library clerk who had unquestioningly accepted my prison ID and lease for the apartment as sufficient identity and proof of residence for issuing a library card.

Lately I was reading everything I could get my hands on about the Civil War, especially in this area of Maryland. Someday I planned to visit the preserved battlefields in the area. Maybe even go to Gettysburg. If I could get permission from my parole officer to leave the state. And if I ever got transportation.

It would be fun to take Kelly's kids there and show them around. She could drive.

Kelly. A lump formed in my throat.

Certainly didn't look like I would be taking Kelly's kids anywhere in the near future. Or ever.

What was going on with her?

There wasn't enough light to read easily, and the words in the book blurred on the page. With a sigh, I wiped my eyes and put it down. I had lighter reading, a book of horror short stories. But the images seemed all too real and too possible to me. I finally got up to do the dishes instead. I decided to take a quick shower and climb into the lumpy but warm bed that came with the apartment.

It sure beat a prison bunk, with its thin fire-resistant crinkly mattress and its single grey woolen blanket, I reminded myself firmly.

Tomorrow was Sunday. On Sunday mornings I usually liked to walk through downtown which had a church on almost every corner. I wasn't about to be a total hypocrite and try to join one, but the families looked solid and content in their Sunday best, and sometimes I could hear the choirs sing.

They didn't usually pay me much mind, maybe a dismissive glance, but with my face all beat up like this, I might be better off staying away. If the parents took a look at me and pulled their kids protectively closer, I'd pretend to ignore it, but it would hurt. Besides, it looked like it was going to be icy and cold.

I had to be to work at midnight for my Monday shift. I should probably get there a bit early, since it didn't look like Kelly was going to be showing up for work.

* * * *

I slept Sunday afternoon, so I would be well-rested for work. The Quality Steel Fabrications plant was only about a fifteen minute walk from my apartment. Whenever I thought about it, I still couldn't quite believe I'd actually landed a job there. They participated in a program that gave tax breaks to companies that gave jobs to parole-eligible prison inmates. I did my best to prove to them that they hadn't made a mistake hiring me.

I packed peanut butter sandwiches in my battered lunchbox and filled its thermos with instant coffee, then left for work. I got there about eleven thirty Sunday night and waited for Jim, the foreman, to tell me how we were going to handle the forklift work tonight.

Ramon, a beefy guy who drove a lift on the four to midnight shift, sat at one of the crude picnic tables between the time-clock and the vending machines that dispensed snacks and a vile dark liquid purported to be coffee. Since his shift hadn't worked Sunday, they must have called him in. Ramon and I had problems in the past, but as far as I was concerned, we'd worked them through. We basically ignored each other most of the time. I hoped we could just let things lie now—I sure didn't need any more trouble than I already had.

Ramon looked surprised when he saw me, but nodded a greeting. I nodded back.

Jim, the foreman, hurried in, his battered clipboard clutched in his one gnarled hand, a chewed pencil stub in the other. He stopped when he saw me.

"Didn't think you were coming in tonight, Jesse," he said, raising his bushy white eyebrows.

Why would he think that? "I'm here," I said.

"So I see." He scratched his chin with the pencil and looked down at me from his height of over six foot five inches. I'm just about six foot.

"I don't think Kelly will be in, though," I said.

"I expect you're right on that. Her dad called the office earlier and said she'd probably be out most of the week." He eyed my bruised face and seemed to be deciding whether to say anything more. "Do you know how she's doing?" he finally asked.

I shrugged. "She's supposed to be doing good, all things considered. But she don't want to see me right now."

"I can't imagine why." Jim shook his head and turned to his clip-board which listed all the jobs, shipments and information he'd need for the shift tonight.

Since they'd called Ramon in, I figured I'd be working my regular duties in the warehouse and the plant floor, with Ramon handling the loading and unloading of trucks. I hadn't needed to come in so early, but that didn't matter.

I put my lunchbox on the table, punched in, hung up my jacket on a hook on the wall, and grabbed my hardhat. A note on the time-clock reminded everyone that most of plant would be shut down next week for retooling. That happened twice a year, and production workers got a week's paid vacation, if they were union members. I'd been working there long enough to be in the union, so I'd be on paid vacation this time. Unless they needed a forklift driver and told me to report. Then I'd work my regular hours and get the vacation at another time.

I sat down across the table from Ramon to wait for the shift to begin.

"They didn't think they'd have a driver at all this shift," he said. "That's why they called me in. I can always use the overtime."

"Really?" I asked. "Jim said Kelly's dad called in, but why did he think I wasn't going to show up?"

Ramon flipped open his lunchbox and pulled out a newspaper. "You see the front page of today's paper?" he asked.

"No." I reached for the paper he was holding out. This couldn't be good.

There I was. Staring right into the camera, my face covered with blood. I looked totally deranged. My hands were pulled behind me, and a burly cop with a grim expression on his face had me by the elbow. It looked like I was trying to break away and he had to actively restrain me.

The caption had my name slightly misspelled, "Jessie Damon," and said I was being arrested on charges of rape, kidnapping, and assault. The brief article below noted that I was on parole for a murder convic-tion and considered armed and dangerous. It primly stated that the paper did not name the victims of sexual assault.

But everybody here at work knew it was Kelly. My status as a paroled murderer was no secret to anyone. The first time I'd made the newspaper had been when I'd been arrested for murder at age sixteen. But that had been in the *Baltimore Sun*, a much bigger paper, and the article had been tucked back on page five or something. Now I was in the news again, and this was on the front page. While I told myself it didn't matter and I shouldn't care, it did bother me.

I remembered the car that had pulled up on Friday when I was being hauled in. It must have been a reporter. With a camera. Probably listening to the police calls and hoping for a dramatic front-page story for the Sunday paper. He—or she—got it.

"My parole officer is gonna love this," I said, rubbing my rough cheek. I still hadn't shaved—I figured it covered some of the bruising, and no one at work cared what anyone looked like as long as the work got done.

"You're not locked up," Ramon said. "Did you post bail?"

I shook my head. "You really think they'd set bail for somebody with my record? On a rape charge? Or that I'd find a bail bondsman willing to post it, even if I could come up with my ten percent?"

"I guess not." He took the paper back. "You look kind of rough in that picture."

"True, that."

"Truth be told, you don't look that much better now."

I grinned and nodded toward the newspaper. "That why Jim thought I wasn't gonna be coming in?"

"Yeah. Everybody figured you'd be in jail." His eyes opened wide. "You didn't *escape,* did you?"

I laughed. "And come into work, where they could just swing by and pick me up? I don't think so. They never charged me."

"But the paper says…"

"I see what the paper says. The reporter overheard the cops talking about those charges. But when Kelly came to and they talked to her, she fingered someone else as the attacker. So they cut me loose."

"Can't they test for DNA or something?"

"I'm sure they will. And it'll come back it wasn't me."

"So who was it? Do you know?"

I shook my head. "No. I tried to go see her, but she wasn't in any mood to talk to me." Slight understatement.

"She still in the hospital?"

"I think so."

"Gonna be okay?"

"As far as I know. But she got a dislocated shoulder or something, so she's gonna be off work for a bit."

The other workers were drifting in. Most of them glanced over and did a double take when they saw me sitting there. Did they all get the Sunday paper?

Ramon leaned forward. "You know that picture was on the news on TV, too?"

Great. Anybody who hadn't seen the paper had probably watched the news.

No point sitting here while everyone gawked. It was a bit early, but I got up and headed back to the charging bay where the electric forklifts were plugged in. Snatching the clipboard from a hook next to my assigned lift, I started on the pre-shift checklist.

Ramon trailed after me and took the clipboard for the larger lift next to mine, the one Kelly usually drove. "What do I do first?" he asked.

"Whatever John tells you. Probably start picking stock and assembling shipments. You get the paperwork from the computer by the dispatcher's office. You know how to read the packing lists?"

"Yeah. But how about the packing line? Don't I have to stay where I can service that?"

"Not until the very end of the shift. It's a little easier than most nights. The plating line's been shut down for the weekend, and it takes almost four hours to get that up. The lacquer line can't start until the platers are running. And the packing line can't pack until there's something on the line *to* pack."

"So I pick stock." He nodded.

"Except when you got a truck to load or unload. Jim'll tell you what to expect."

"Thanks." Ramon swung up onto his seat and backed out.

The whistle blew to start the shift. Machinery rumbled to life. Sparks flew, presses set into their thunderous rhythm, and the air filled with the pungent odors of oil and hot steel.

Back in the warehouse, I rearranged a few pallets of open steel rings that would be welded together to make baskets for tree roots at some point. The root baskets weren't some of the most elegant products Quality Steel Fabrications made, but they were easy and profitable, and we made lots of them. Welding them was the first job I'd been put on when I'd started here.

As I replaced the pallets, larger rings in the back to the smaller ones in the front, I noticed something light-colored on the floor behind another pallet. I got off the lift and picked it up.

It was a woman's purse. What the hell was that doing back here? I knew there were a number of women who worked in the plant who might have business back in the warehouse, but they were all production workers, like Kelly. I'd never seen one of them carry a purse to work. If they had stuff they didn't want to carry in their pockets, like cell phones, it probably ended up in their lunchboxes, just like with the men.

And I'd *never* noticed a production worker with makeup.

The ladies in the office dressed in nice clothes and carried purses, but I doubted any of them would come back here. A hard hat would squash their hairdos, and I didn't know whether anyone in dress shoes would be permitted back here. We all wore steel-toed boots.

I debated looking inside it, but decided it wasn't my place to do that. I tucked it behind the seat of the forklift, figuring I could give it to Jim, or if I didn't see him, hand it in to the timekeeper when she arrived at seven o'clock to get paperwork ready for the day shift. She had a lost-and-found box in her office.

I brought supplies for the machine operators from the warehouse and removed full pallets of completed parts. Most of the workers glanced curiously at me as I passed, but we were busy working and the noise level of the shop floor didn't permit casual conversation. That suited me fine, under the circumstances.

The plating room, though, where I'd worked before I was assigned to be a forklift driver, was relaxed as the operators brought the electro-platers, their rows of tanks stretching into the gloom, up to production speed. The overhead carriers, left empty over the weekend, hovered over the tanks, began their endless lurch and dip dance as they were set in motion. As each empty set of hooks paused in front of the operator, who attached a dull grey piece to them and waited for the next set of hooks. When they were operating at full capacity, keeping up with the loading and unloading the shelves and cabinets from the overhead carriers was a constant challenge for the operators, but now they only had to load the line until the first ones made it all the way through all the plating tanks and back to the front of the squat behemoths. It would take much of the shift before the first gleaming pieces returned to the front.

Hank, the plating room group lead, stood with his clipboard in his beefy hand, checking the work list.

"Jesse," he shouted over the sound of the lurching machinery. "Come into the office. We got to go over the work orders."

I eased the forklift to a stop next to the office and followed him in. The office was stifling hot. Hank was pulling dirty papers from equally grimed file folders. "Damn new system," he muttered. "I can't figure out what the hell we're supposed to be doing here."

Some enthusiastic new junior executive hire had implemented a new computer tracking system for both inventory and work flow. It was supposed to let everyone know exactly what needed to be done when, what parts and supplies were running low and what we had in stock to fill orders. It probably worked perfectly well from the point of view of the office workers, but as far as I could see, it just complicated the work for those of us who actually had to do the work. Instructions that had been scrawled on one sheet of paper were now on five-page printouts. Some of it was almost indecipherable even to reasonably intelligent people who could read well. For years, the only requirements for hiring laborers had been a strong back and a willingness to work hard, regardless of educational level. And the best of the workers, those who understood the jobs and the machinery and could get things done, were promoted. Hank was one of the old-school group leaders.

I owed Hank. He'd been decent to me when I'd first been assigned to operate a plater, showing me how to do the work. I'd been a probationary employee, and he'd given me a chance to learn the ropes. I knew he had trouble reading, so I took the papers and sorted through them.

"Oven shelves are top priority," I told him, taking his pen to circle the part names and numbers so he could pick them out easily. "And they aren't fussy, so we should run them until the platers are going good. Then maybe start one of the platers on those big grills—I don't know what they're for, really, but they need a fair number of them. If you get far enough along, you could start those breaker boxes, but they don't ship until Wednesday, so they're not a rush."

Hank nodded and rubbed a thick finger against his nose. The tattoos on the backs of his hands glistened with sweat.

He shifted his massive weight uneasily and peered at me from under his shaggy eyebrows. "I know it ain't really none of my business, Jesse, but you know, I been working with Kelly for years. I was real upset to hear somebody'd done that to her."

I took a deep breath. "I know what you mean."

He squinted at me, his small eyes piercing. "*Did* you have anything to do with it?"

"No. I wasn't anywhere near her when it happened."

"I thought you two was an item."

Wiping my hands on my blue jeans, I said, "Not really. We saw each other sometimes, but you know, her dad got out of prison, and he was using her place as his reported residence. I can't associate with convicted felons, and he's sure as hell a convicted felon, too. So I was staying away."

He nodded. "Was her dad hanging around a lot?"

"I think so."

"And how about them bikers he rides with?"

"Them too."

"Don't they got a clubhouse up in the hills? Out behind that excavating business some of them run? Nobody cares what they do out there."

"I don't know about the excavating business, but Kelly did say they had someplace outside town they could go. I think Kelly wasn't real happy having them around her kids so much."

"Why hang out at Kelly's place in town? That's just asking for trouble."

"Wondered that myself. I didn't think Old Buckles, her dad, was on home detention, but sometimes the parole officer springs that on you at the last minute. Then he'd have to wear an ankle bracelet, be in his little circle around the transmitter at Kelly's place for maybe twelve hours a day, probably like seven PM to seven AM."

Hank shook his shaggy head. "You think it might have been one of them did her?"

"Might be. But I'd have thought Old Buckles would have put the fear of the Lord into them. He still thinks of Kelly as his little girl."

"Some of them guys, they get real high. They don't think. And they certainly aren't afraid of the Lord. Or anyone else."

I nodded. I knew some people like that.

"Well." Hank gathered up the papers. "Anything I can do to help the little lady, let me know."

Not too many people would think of Kelly as being a "little lady" any more than they would "little girl," but I guess that next to Hank's hulking form, she was.

"If I hear of anything," I said, "you'll be the first to know. But I doubt I will. I'm kind of out of the loop."

Most of the shift had their lunch from exactly 4:00 to 4:18 a.m., while those working on a continuous operation, like the platers or packing line, took staggered lunches when they could be relieved. I had no desire to sit down with anyone else, so I kept working through the regular lunch and told John I'd grab mine at the picnic table back in the shipping room when I'd made sure all the work was caught up.

About four forty-five, I picked up my lunchbox from near the time-clock and went to find Jim to tell him I was going to lunch if it was okay with him.

He was deep in conversation with the security guard who patrolled a regular path through the plant and grounds. I eased the forklift over and waited for them to finish talking. Although we were away from the production floor and the din of machinery was muted, I couldn't hear any of what they were saying.

I got down to talk to Jim as the security guard started to leave.

He did a double take as he passed the forklift. Reaching behind the seat, he lifted the purse.

"Where the hell did you get *that?*" he asked.

Jim stared at the purse and then turned to look at me.

"Back in the warehouse," I said. *Why the hell hadn't I turned it in when I first found it?* "It was behind a pallet, by the root basket rings."

The security guard examined the purse but didn't open it. "And why didn't you give it to somebody?"

I knew I should have. I said, "I was gonna give it to Jim at the end of the shift. Or turn it in to the lost and found in the timekeeper's office."

"Sure looks like the one I was telling you to keep an eye out for," the guard said to Jim. "Fancy it turning up just like that, after being missing for two days."

Jim shook his head.

"Be interesting to see if the car keys are still in it," the guard said. "The owner can look when she reports for work in the morning. Mind if I lock it up in an office?"

"Sounds like a plan to me," Jim said.

We watched him walk away, purse dangling from his bony hand.

Jim turned to look down at me. "Did you really find it in the warehouse?" he asked.

This whole thing couldn't look good. I swallowed. "Yes."

"Did you open it up?"

"No. I thought about it, find out who it belonged to, but then I decided it was better to let somebody in authority look for ID or something."

"So you don't know whose it is, or if it's a wallet in it or keys or anything."

"No, sir."

Jim sighed. "It went missing a few days ago. Probably from the office. Or maybe the ladies' room up there. And yesterday, the owner's car was stolen from in front of her house. I don't suppose you know anything about that, either, do you?"

"No, sir. What kind of car was it?"

"A fairly new BMW. Her husband just caught a glimpse of someone driving it away. A skinny white guy with brown hair."

That description came uncomfortably close to me. "I don't have a driver's license."

Jim cast a disgusted look at me. "You think anybody who'd steal a car would be worried about driving it without a license?"

When he put it like that, I had to say, "No, sir."

I wasn't hungry any more, but I knew I should eat. I drove off and parked the lift back in shipping. I had no sooner poured the coffee into the cup and unwrapped the sandwich when someone slammed a couple of cans of soda and a bag from a takeout burger joint on the table next to me.

Aaron. He was a kid who worked the packing line. When he showed up for work. He was a drug abuser and often made my life miserable, trying to get me to hook him up with sources of meth or crack. Or both. He thought I was connected because of my record, and I hadn't been able to convince him I wasn't a drug user and never had been. He just didn't believe me.

He was another skinny white guy with brown hair. Real skinny.

With his attendance record, he should have been fired. The only explanation I could come up with for why he hadn't been was because he was a police informant, and the company had been asked to keep him on. Not long ago, a fairly sophisticated drug and fake ID distribution had been uncovered in the plant, with the contraband going out shrink-wrapped and hidden in shipments on the trucks. It had been orchestrated by an executive. The management seemed to discount that little fact and was more interested in what we laborers might be doing in the shop than what might be going on upstairs in the offices.

"Hey, Jesse," Aaron said, slipping his pencil-thin legs over the picnic table bench and plopping down beside me.

I certainly didn't feel like talking to anybody, much less him, so I just looked at him, then turned back to my lunch and started eating.

"So what happened to Kelly?" He pulled a cold greasy burger out of the bag and dumped some limp, slimy fries right on the grungy planks of the table top.

Maybe if I ignored him, he would leave me alone.

Fat chance. "So now you're not talking to me?" he said. "Why? 'Cause she beat you up? Is that what happened to your face?"

I wanted to get done with my lunch and get back to work, even if I cut my break short. I shoved an entire half of the sandwich in my mouth.

That's not a good idea when it's dry bread with plenty of peanut butter on it. I choked on it and started coughing. Reaching for my coffee, I knocked the cup to the floor.

"Hey, man. Have this." Aaron opened one of his cans of soda and shoved it toward me. Then he started pounding me on the back. "You want I should try the Heimlich maneuver?"

"No!" I managed to gasp out. I coughed again. He stood up. I grabbed the soda and downed a big swallow, washing down the lump stuck in my throat. "I'm okay now. Don't touch me!"

"Okay." Aaron sat down again. "You want the other soda?"

"No thanks. There's still some left in this can." What I had didn't taste like any soda I'd ever had. I looked at the can. Grape soda. What adult drank grape soda?

"Want me to get you some water?" he asked, starting to get up again.

"No. I'm fine."

Aaron grinned. "You don't *look* fine. But maybe it's just your face. What *did* happen to you? Wasn't Kelly, was it?"

I sighed. After he'd been willing to help me, I couldn't continue to just ignore him. "No. Got my face slammed into the hood of a cop car."

"Must have been pretty hard."

"It was."

He laughed. "Did it dent the hood?"

I had to smile at the thought of leaving a dent in the hood of Montgomery's otherwise pristine ride. "Didn't look, so I don't know."

"So it didn't have anything to do with Kelly?"

"Nah."

"Or when you went to settle with the guy who did her?"

"I don't even know who that was. Yet."

"What *did* happen to her?"

"I dunno. I wasn't there."

"Who was?"

"If I wasn't there, how am I supposed to know?"

A depraved, hungry look came over his face. "You think she really got raped?"

My gut twisted. "That's what I heard."

"You gonna do anything about it?"

"What'd ya mean?"

"She's *your* woman, ain't she? So you gonna go take care of whoever moved in on you?"

I shook my head. "First of all, she ain't *my* woman. We're not married or engaged or anything. No commitment." My mind reeled. Married? Me? Where did that thought come from?

Taking a deep breath, I told him the same thing I'd told the bikers. "She's her own person. She can do what she wants with anybody she wants to do it with."

"Including screwing them?"

"If she wants to. But that don't give nobody the right to do anything to her she don't want them to."

"So you gonna take care of it?"

"Don't you listen?" But I knew the drugs had addled his mind to the point he forgot a lot of things. "I don't even know *who* it was did it. So how'm I gonna do anything about it?"

"She didn't tell you?"

"She don't want to see me."

Aaron pondered that for a few minutes. Or zoned out. Hard to tell.

I retrieved the cup to my thermos from the floor. The spilled coffee soaked right into the old wood planks, so I didn't bother trying to wipe it up. I gathered up the wrapping from my sandwich and tossed it into the trash barrel.

"Say." Aaron shook himself and turned his bleary eyes on me.

"What?"

"You know Old Buckles, the biker?"

"Yeah. He's Kelly's dad. He's just got out of prison. He's using Kelly's place as his approved residence for parole.'"

"Really. Anyhow, he been asking about you."

"What about me?"

"When you get off work, where you stay at, that kind of stuff."

"He could just ask Kelly."

"Maybe he don't want Kelly to know he's asking." Aaron scratched a scab on the back of his hand. It bled, but he didn't seem to notice.

I snapped the top on my lunchbox shut. "No secrets about my work schedule. Easy enough to find out. He could even ask me."

"You seen him?"

"Yeah. The other night at the hospital. He can find me whenever he wants to. My schedule's pretty predictable." When I wasn't being hauled off to jail, that is. "He don't need to ask you."

"You'd think so." Aaron looked around and lowered his voice. "But he *paid* me to tell him."

"Paid you? How much?"

"Couple of rocks of crack."

"You'd better stay away from them bikers. The Predators are in a whole different league than you."

Aaron smirked. "That's what *you* think."

I really didn't want to know what Aaron was getting involved with now. Just so long as it didn't have anything to do with me. "What did you tell him?"

"Where you live at. Like you say, it ain't no secret. And that you get off of work at eight a.m."

"So should I expect him to be waiting for me when I punch out this morning?"

"I don't think so. Unless it rains."

"What's rain got to do with it?"

"If it's raining or too cold, he can't work. He's got to keep a job for parole. He's working on a crew out where they're building that new bridge. They start work at seven. Good job. He don't want to mess that up."

For once, Aaron was probably on target. Parole people came down hard on people who lost their jobs. Sometimes they got locked up again.

"I got some new contacts," he said. "People taking pretty good care of me. You interested in making some extra money?"

"No."

I went over and climbed back on my forklift.

"Jesse?" Aaron called after me.

I was tempted to keep going, but I turned back to him. "What?"

"You gonna hook me up with a supplier?"

I was pretty sure I knew, but I asked, "Supplier of what?"

"You know. Meth. Or crack."

"How about them new contacts? They can't help you out there?"

He looked around. "Eventually, they said. But not right now."

"Hope you're not getting in over your head, buddy."

He looked surprised. "Me? I've just started with them. They need a little time before they can trust me."

I looked at Aaron's slouching stick-thin figure, his blood-shot eyes, and rotting teeth. Not to mention the scabs on his face and hands. Even if I was wrong about him being a police informant, *nobody* in their right mind would trust him.

"Only thing I'll hook you up with is Narcotics Anonymous. I'll take you to a meeting if you want."

A crafty look crept into his narrowed eyes. "I didn't know you went to NA."

"I don't."

"Then how you gonna take me to a meeting?"

"No problem finding out about the meetings. And anyone can go."

"*Do* you go sometimes?"

"Nope."

"Why not?"

"'Cause I don't use."

Aaron looked me up and down. "Okaaaay…" he said.

I had an uneasy feeling he thought he knew something about me. Even if he was wrong, he could cause problems for me.

CHAPTER 6

As I got out of work, I scanned the street for bikers, but all I saw were cars, most of them were parked and empty. A cold wind blew down the street, and a weak sun was trying to peer through the scattered cloud cover.

One car, a late-model silver Lexus, peeled out of the parking lot and skidded to a stop beside me.

"Hey, Jesse!" Aaron shouted out the open window. Last time I'd seen him behind the wheel, he'd been driving a beaten up blue pickup. "Want a ride home?"

"No." I eyed the vehicle. "And where the hell did you get *that*?"

Aaron smirked at me. "Let's just say I borrowed it."

"Yeah? And who lent it to you?"

"Some of my new business partners. They think it's important that I look prosperous if I'm gonna work for them. You know, like they don't got to go scraping for cash."

A shower and some decent clothes would go a long way toward that for Aaron, I thought, without making him look like a car thief. But I didn't say anything.

"So you gonna climb in or not?" he asked.

"Not."

"Why not?"

"I got no idea where you got that car. I'm not gonna take any chances of being caught riding in a stolen vehicle."

"Aw, Jesse. It's legit. It's *cold* out. I can give you a ride home."

"Thanks, but no thanks."

Aaron shrugged, rolled up the window, and laid rubber as he took off.

I flipped up my hood, slipped my hands in my pockets and turned toward my apartment.

Another car was parked by the curb, a driver behind the wheel. The car was a puke-green hybrid gas/electric model. The windows were tinted, and I couldn't see the driver well, or whether there were additional occupants. It started up as I passed it.

Uneasy, I didn't look back at it. It didn't look like an unmarked cop car—what cop would drive a puke-green hybrid? More likely they picked something like the black Lincoln Belkins and Montgomery were using, or a four wheel drive SUV. But they confiscated all kinds of vehicles when they found drugs and used them for a while, so the possibility was always there. It made no noise as it glided along beside me.

The muscles in my shoulders and neck tightened. I stopped and backed up against a wall to let it pass.

It slowed down.

I glanced around. I could turn back the way I'd come or step down an alley. But the sun was now washing the sidewalks with feeble morning light, and the driver would have no trouble seeing where I went. I made sure my hands were in plain sight. If it *was* a cop, I for sure didn't want anyone thinking I was going for a weapon.

The car pulled over to the curb, slid past a fire hydrant and stopped. The door opened.

A cop wouldn't have worried about parking next to the fire hydrant.

The driver was a *she*. A very attractive she. Petite, blond, a flawlessly made-up face. And wearing spike heels and a fake fur coat. Or maybe it was real fur, although that didn't seem to go with the hybrid.

Nobody I knew. I shifted from one foot to the other, still careful to keep my hands where they could be seen. She came directly toward me. Somebody from the parole office? A social worker?

Smiling, she said. "Jesse Damon?"

She obviously knew exactly who I was, so I saw no point in denying it. "Yeah."

"My name is Carissa Daniles," she said, holding out her hand for me to shake.

Not knowing what else to do, I wiped my hand on my jeans to get some of the oil and dirt off it and took her hand. It was soft and smooth.

She tossed her multi-colored blond hair back over her shoulders and smiled again, showing more teeth than I would have thought a human mouth could hold. "I'm with the *Rothsburg Register*," she said.

Rothsburg Register. That was the paper that had carried my picture on the front page yesterday.

I couldn't think of a response to that.

"I was hoping you'd talk to me a little," she said.

"I got nothing to say," I answered.

She tilted her chin in and looked up at me with big brown eyes from under thick dark eyelashes. "Oh, I'm sure you have lots you could tell me."

I scratched my cheek. My beard was reaching the itchy stage. Time to shave or decide I actually was growing a beard. "I dunno what."

When she stepped closer to me, I caught a clean, flowery soap scent. Maybe it was perfume. Her smell was tantalizing, not at all like the hot steel and oil smell of the factory. Or the sweaty body odor I was sure she'd pick up if she got too close to me. I leaned away from her, but I had the wall at my back.

Her voice was a soft purr. "How about we go get breakfast someplace?"

I was on a tight budget that didn't lend itself to spur of the moment restaurant meals. And would she expect me to pay for her? "No, thanks."

She was so close her fluffy red scarf touched my jacket. Her voice was soft and low. "My treat."

"No, ma'am. I can't accept that."

"Expense account," she said.

Did that mean the newspaper was paying for it? Still, she had to want something from me, or she wouldn't be offering.

"No, thanks." I couldn't remember being this close to any woman but Kelly since I'd been a little kid. I felt damp sweat beading on my back.

"We could just go for a cup of coffee." She took hold of the front of my unzipped jacket. "Just you and me."

"I don't think so." Was she trying to set me up? "And I think I'd better be going, ma'am."

She frowned. Her perfectly made up face was just as pretty as when she smiled. "Why not? You can't tell me you're afraid of me?"

Maybe I was. But what I said was, "I almost just got arrested on rape charges. That can't come as any surprise to you. I'm damn sure not going anyplace, 'just you and me,' with a woman I don't know."

She stepped back and did that flip thing with her hair again. "Okay. How about a cup of coffee at Starbucks? That's plenty public."

I'd never been in a Starbucks. And I *knew* I should say no. But she smiled again and looked up at me with those big brown eyes and stepped close so her intriguing scent filled my nostrils. "Please? I won't take much of your time."

"Okay."

"Great." She took my sleeve and pulled me across the sidewalk. "I'll drive."

I stopped short. "I'm *not* getting in that car with you."

She frowned. "How are we going to get to Starbucks?"

"Tell me where it is, and I'll meet you there." Unless I came to my senses on the walk over and went home instead.

Her bright pink lips formed a pout. "It's all the way across town."

I almost said, "So?" but that might sound rude. "There's a McDonald's a few blocks over," I said. "How about I meet you over there?"

She reached up with a pink fingernail that matched her lips and touched my cheek, stubble and all. "Sure you're not going to run out on me?"

I shifted from one foot to the other. "I'll be there."

"Okay. If you promise. See you there!" She gave me one last look from under her hedgerow of eyelashes and hurried to her car.

McDonald's sold any size coffee for a dollar. Even I could afford that kind of splurge.

When I walked up, she was waiting at the door. Gesturing toward a booth in the back, she said, "I already got our coffee. And a couple of breakfast burritos."

A pile of at least a half dozen sat on the tray with two large coffees. My stomach growled.

What the hell was I doing here? With an attractive woman who worked for the local newspaper?

I was aware of how stupid I was being, but I found myself following my nose as she wound her way back to the booth, her tantalizing scent lingering in the air.

"Have a few of the burritos," she said, taking off her coat. "I can't possibly eat more than one. And I shouldn't eat that. Have to watch my girlish figure, you know."

She giggled and ran her hands down the tight-fitting top she wore. It was hard not to stare. She was so *skinny.* Like Aaron. I wondered briefly if she did drugs, too. But her skin was clear, and her brown eyes were sharp and bright, even this early in the morning.

I shrugged off my jacket and laid it on the seat next to me.

Carissa slipped into the booth across from me and smiled again. She closed her eyes and bowed her head. I wouldn't have pegged her as the type to say grace before meals—Mrs. Coleman had always insisted on a moment of silence for thanksgiving before we were allowed to dive into our food—but what did I know? I sat mesmerized, staring at her.

Her arms were so thin they looked like they might snap if anything touched them, the elbows forming sharp angled points. I thought about Kelly's solid muscles on her sturdy frame.

Her eyes still closed, Carissa gave a huge sigh, her chest heaving. I saw she *did* have breasts, small pointy ones. They certainly weren't the luxurious soft expanse Kelly had. What would they feel like if I reached over and touched them?

Hugging her might feel like I was holding a bunch of clothes hangers.

What was the matter with me? I had to stop thinking like this. I grinned, thinking of a bundle of clothes hangers under her shirt. It was a good thing we *were* in a public place. I blushed and shoved the strands of hair that had escaped from my hair tie back from my face.

Carissa's eyes opened, and she shook herself. "Mediating," she said. "Seeking my inner muse."

I had no idea what she was talking about. It didn't sound like saying grace, though.

She slid further into the booth. Her bony knees brushed against mine. I quickly moved my legs so they were tucked off to the side, but hers followed and settled gently against mine. Was she *trying* to touch my leg with hers?

I hadn't had much contact with women in the last twenty years or so, but I'd had plenty of contact with crazies. Crazies tend to get locked up a lot. And the alarm bells were going off in my head.

She leaned forward, once again filling my nose with her scent. I tried to concentrate on how good the coffee smelled instead.

"Now," she said, "can I ask you a few questions?"

"I guess." A thought that had been nagging at the back of my mind pushed to the forefront. "Are you the one who put that picture on the front page of the paper?"

Her laugh sounded like breaking glass. "Yes, of course. Good picture, don't you think?"

I found it humiliating, but I didn't think she'd understand if I tried to tell her that. "Not really."

She pouted. "I thought it was good. It just simmered of violence, some just past and the potential of more to come."

Maybe. But *I* was the one who had looked violent. Not the image I wanted to project. Pretty obvious she hadn't taken how it felt to be the one in the picture. The memory made me flinch. I took a deep breath and said, "The caption said I was arrested for rape and kidnapping and assault."

She gave a little smile, like we were talking about the weather or something equally mundane. "Well, weren't you?"

"If I had been, I wouldn't be here right now. I was never charged. Just questioned and cut loose." I skipped over the night in jail.

"Oh." She took a sip of her coffee. "Sorry about that. I was going by what the detective said."

And she hadn't bothered to check her facts. That wasn't very professional for a reporter.

"So," she said. "What can you tell me about the, ah, *incident* that lead to that arrest?"

The coffee was good, much better than my usual instant, but there was a harsh taste in my mouth when I took a drink. "Not a damn thing."

"Wasn't the victim your girlfriend?"

I was beginning to get used to the stabbing pain that twisted my gut every time I thought about Kelly and the rape. "I know her. And I spent some time over her place. But no, she's not my *girlfriend*."

"That's not what *I* heard." She smiled and gave me that look out of the side of her eyes. "A big handsome man like you? Why not?"

I felt heat rise in my face, and I wondered if I was blushing. *Was she flirting with me?*

I didn't *do* flirting. Neither did Kelly. Why would this woman be interested in me? Despite what she said, I was pretty damn sure I wasn't her idea of a "big handsome man." She was trying to soften me up and confuse me, so I'd blurt out uncensored answers to her probing and possibly personal questions. Although I had to admit her method was infinitely more pleasing that Belkins' and Montgomery's interrogation routines, I was familiar with the basic techniques. I wondered if Montgomery had ever considered bringing in a sexy female cop as his partner to help him ask questions when he needed answers. Sure would beat an alcoholic, burnt-out cop with a quick hands and a quicker temper.

She raised her eyebrows and pursed her lips. "I'm waiting…"

I took a swallow of coffee. "Kelly and I work together. Sometimes we spend time together outside of work."

Licking her lips, Carissa asked, "Have sex?" I looked at her. She looked like a model in a magazine cosmetics ad. Or a movie star on a poster. Not somebody I could relate to. "Sometimes. But I don't see that it's really anyone else's business. We're both adults, and we're both single."

"But she's been *raped*. You can't tell me most men don't have a rape fantasy."

I bent the thin coffee stirrer as I considered. Where was this going? *The Rothsburg Register* wasn't one of those supermarket tabloids that traded on sex and scandals, mostly made up. I pulled my legs back under my seat.

"I don't know about most men. I don't." I swallowed the last of the coffee, put down the cup and started to slide out of the booth.

"Why are you leaving?" she pouted. "Didn't you know that some women have fantasies of being raped?"

"No, I didn't." I got to my feet. My first instinct had been right. I didn't like where she was headed, and I didn't like where it was ending up. And I didn't like that I'd let myself be manipulated.

The catchall expression, "ain't right in the head" came to mind. Her, definitely. Me, possibly. I had to get out of there.

"I think you're putting me on. You can't be as naïve as all that."

"You'd be surprised," I said, heading for the door.

"Do you mind if I contact you again?" she called after me.

I didn't answer that.

Too bad about the breakfast burritos.

CHAPTER 7

The next morning the bikers were waiting for me when I got off work.

About ten of them lined the street. The headlamps glistened off the asphalt which was wet from an early morning rain, and the engines of the choppers growled. As usual, I was one of the last of my shift to leave. The few stragglers just ahead of me glanced quickly toward the bikers, then away, and hurried to the parking lot.

Old Buckles sat on his trike in the front of the group, his beefy arms crossed in front of his chest. Despite the damp chill, his jacket was unzipped. The other Predators leaned on their bikes or shielded their smokes from the wind. All wore leather jackets with club colors.

Funky Joe revved his engine and scowled in my direction, but he didn't say anything. His jaw was swollen, and his eye black.

I stopped in front of Old Buckles and looked him in the eye. "You looking for me?"

He grinned, showing his blackened teeth. "Yeah."

Glancing around me, I said, "Can we move it a little bit away from the plant entrance?"

"You afraid we're gonna freak out the employees?"

"You probably already done that."

He laughed. "Yeah. One of those little office worker ladies wouldn't get out of her car. Waited until a few men were walking by and went in with them."

"Can you blame her?"

"Guess not. But we been here for a little while already. Why should we move now?"

"Look, you know how hard it is to get a job when you've got felonies. I got a good job. I'd hate to have them think you guys were gonna come around on a regular basis to see me. Might make them look for a reason to fire me."

He nodded. "I wouldn't have gotten the construction job I got now if I didn't know the crew chief. He'd done time with me a few years back. He knows I don't mind working."

"It won't make no difference to you guys if we move a few blocks down. But it could make a big difference to me."

"And why should I care about that?"

"Same reason the crew chief went to bat for you and got you the job."

Old Buckles sat there grinning. He was enjoying this little exchange. "Which was?"

"Give a break to a fellow con who can't catch one no way else."

He threw back his head and laughed again. "You done talked me into it. How about the park down by the railroad tracks? Throw a bit of a scare into all the druggies down there trying to score."

"That'll work."

"Course, that's if they've crawled out of their holes yet."

I nodded. "True, that."

"You wanna ride down there?"

I didn't, and I knew I there were a few problems with that idea, not the least of which was the possibility of being seen by the police, but all I had going now was bravado and Old Buckle's precariously benevolent attitude toward me.

He inched forward in his seat, and I swung up behind him.

"Hope nobody don't see me giving a ride to somebody who ain't no wearing colors," he said, revving the throttle and releasing the brake.

That made two of us who hoped nobody saw us.

We roared the few blocks toward the park, the other bikes following us. They pulled up over the curb and the weedy lawn, onto the cracked blacktop of the basketless basketball court.

I climbed off and brushed my hair back.

Someone passed a blunt to Old Buckles. He took a deep drag and gestured toward me, coughing and re-inhaling the smoke.

"No thanks."

He narrowed his eyes suspiciously, "Why not?"

"You have any idea how long that stays in your system if they test your piss? Or in your hair?"

"So who's gonna piss you?"

"My PO, for starters."

Old Buckles spit onto the pavement and looked at me. "I still haven't figured this whole thing out yet," he said.

"Oh?" I wasn't about to offer any ideas.

"Kelly, she said she wasn't gonna be nobody's old lady. Girlfriend, maybe, but not a real solid thing. She seemed to take a shining to you."

I nodded, turning to look toward the railroad tracks I liked nothing better than spending the evening with Kelly and her kids, fixing dinner, playing games, reading stories to the kids. Except, of course, going to bed with her. I tried to keep my agony from showing on my face. From what I knew of Old Buckles, I was pretty sure he'd never understand what Kelly and I had going.

He shifted on his seat. "So I don't get why you'd tell somebody else they could screw her."

I jerked around to face Old Buckles squarely again struggling to keep my voice from raising to a shout. "What?"

"Black Rose—you know Black Rose?"

Cautiously, I said, "I know who she is. But not I don't know her well or anything."

"According to her, you know her a whole hell of a lot better than that. She says her old man, Razorback, and you agreed that you could screw each other's ladies."

"That's news to me," I said, shaking my head and trying to think straight. "Kelly'd never go for that." Even if I did. Which I couldn't imagine myself doing.

"Well, that's part of what I can't figure out." His jaw jutted out stubbornly, and his eyebrows furrowed over his glowering eyes. "Kelly says Razorback never said nothing like that to her. But he was pretty high. And she'd maybe been drinking. He just started ripping her shirt off, and when she said leave her alone, he smacked her a few times." His face hardened.

Taking a deep breath and choking back anguish I said, "Sure wish I'd been there. Would have come out different."

He raised his eyebrows and stroked his braided beard. "Why the hell weren't you there?"

"Where's 'there'?"

"Kelly's house. Living room. Kids had gone with their pop for the weekend."

"You know I'm on parole. Trying not to violate. Associating with convicted felons—which is exactly what I'm doing now—is grounds for violation. So Kelly and I decided to cool it while you're living there."

He glared at me. "What kind of a wuss are you, worrying so much about violating that you stay away from your girlfriend?"

"The kind of wuss who did twenty years and has close to another twenty backup time."

He grinned. "Didn't like being locked up, huh?"

"Nope." *Who did?*

"It ain't so bad. I been doing nickels and dimes ever since I can remember."

"Mine's been straight time. Since I was sixteen."

He looked me up and down. "I can see where you might not want to go back. 'Specially if you might never see light of day again."

"You got that right."

Shrugging, he said, "Why would Black Rose say you and Razorback made that deal if you didn't?"

"I couldn't tell you that. This is the first time I heard about it."

"She says she got the best end of the deal."

"Huh?" Had she actually told everybody I'd had sex with her? My muscles tensed, and I turned my head again to stare down the tracks. Where was this going? I fought to keep my shock surprise from showing on my face. Wouldn't do to let this crowd know it was hitting me hard. They made a habit of exploiting weakness whenever they saw it.

"Black Rose says she never had it so good, that you're great in bed."

I turned to face him again and felt the blood drain from my face. My jaws clenched so I had trouble getting any words out. "She said *what*?"

"That you know what a woman likes and don't mind taking your time to make sure she's getting it." He raised his eyebrows and grinned. "She's more used to guys who just take what they think what they got coming to them. Like Razorback done with Kelly."

Was there any way to make Old Buckles believe me? "Didn't never go there." What else was she making up? And *why*? Kelly was the only woman I'd ever had sex with. She'd had to show me what she liked. And while I certainly loved to take the time to do what Kelly liked, I wasn't about to go screwing other women.

Especially not biker chicks. They had notoriously possessive boy-friends, although it was more about control than jealousy. These bikers were serious about their women being their property, to screw or lend out whenever they felt like it. I couldn't imagine thinking that way about another human being. Especially Kelly.

"You don't got to worry about nobody's reputation or any of that shit with me," Old Buckles said. "'Specially not if he gave you the go-ahead."

Shaking my head, I said, "I've never even *talked* to Black Rose. Or Razorback."

He ignored that. "What I'm wondering," he said, "is did Black Rose tell him what a great lay you are? Was he jealous? Maybe took it out on Kelly? To show Black Rose what a bad ass he can be."

This conversation was getting seriously out of control. "I didn't tell Razorback it was okay to screw Kelly. And I never 'did' Black Rose."

"You really expect me to believe that?"

I needed more time to think this whole thing out, so I tried to change the subject. "Where's Razorback now?"

The grin was back. "That's what we've been wondering. Nobody's seen him. Not even Black Rose. She says his bike's still in the garage. Not like a biker to take off without the bike."

"So he's gone off somewhere?"

"Seems like it. Not smart, though. He'll be in trouble when they do find him."

That was familiar territory to me. "Parole violation?" I asked.

Old Buckles shrugged. "I'm not sure about that. But he's a registered sex offender. That means he's got to let them know where he's staying all the time. What with this stuff with Kelly, you *know* they're aware that he's not at his registered address. And he hasn't filed for a change of address. That'd show up on the registry within a day. Rose looked it up."

"He got any family or anything? They might know where he's got to."

"Nobody we know of. We're wondering if *you* knew what happened to him."

Shaking my head, I said, "No idea. I wouldn't even recognize him if I saw him."

"Him and Black Rose run a little excavating firm. Trenches for residential sewer connections and stuff like that. Although I think Black Rose does most of it. I know she runs the backhoe. And keeps the books."

That was interesting, but I didn't see it was particularly relevant. I nodded.

"It's up on the same property where the clubhouse is."

Once again, I nodded, still not quite following where this was leading.

He scratched under his braided beard. "If Razorback don't put in an appearance one of these days, you planning to move in with her and help with the business? And even if he does, he's gonna be locked up."

That one took me by surprise. "I don't even *know* Black Rose. I sure as hell ain't gonna be moving in with some woman I don't know. Or go stay up at where you guys got your clubhouse. Ain't my style. And I got a good steady job I don't want to quit. Don't think my PO'd be happy with any of that. Not to mention me." The idea of moving in with Kelly and the kids had occurred to me a few times. It wasn't gonna happen any time soon, but it appealed to me on lots of levels. But hitching up like that with Black Rose? No way.

"I'm still trying to figure this out," he said. "So don't you be putting me on. If you're gonna be doing that, I want to know. My little girl, she been hurt enough. More than enough. Don't see it myself, but I know she used to have a soft spot for you. I think she still might. Don't you be playing with her feelings if you don't want to answer to me."

Could he be right about Kelly still caring? I turned away from him again to hide the tears that began to gather in my eyes and confusion that must be evident on my face. The brief glints of sunlight that managed to peek through the clouds glinted off the worn railroad tracks. If Kelly really thought I'd made some kind of deal with Razorback, it was no wonder she was mad at me.

But she hadn't *asked* me or anything. Just assumed what Black Rose told her was the truth. What kind of relationship could we have if she was willing to believe any sordid story anybody told her about me? Most of the time, I expected people to believe the worst of me. It went with the territory. But until all this came down, I'd thought Kelly thought different.

A siren sounded in the distance. I swiped my sleeve across my eyes and glanced at the other bikers. They'd all heard it, too, and were tossing beer cans and cigarette butts into the scraggly weeds around the pavement. The roaches got pinched out and slipped into pockets.

A puke-green car pulled up to the curb. Carissa got out of the driver's seat, camera in her hand.

Old Buckles glowered in her direction. "Who the hell's that bitch?"

"A reporter from the newspaper," I said.

She raised the camera and appeared to be taking pictures. I turned sideways, hoping I could avoid a repeat of last Sunday's front page story.

"I ought to grab that camera and shove it down her throat," Old Buckles said, starting to swing off the trike.

The siren grew louder. The Predators who had dismounted climbed back on their bikes. Old Buckles paused and then settled back in his seat.

"Bitch," he muttered under his breath. Then he turned to me. "You wanna get out of here with us?"

I considered. Somebody must have called the cops about the unsavory group hanging out in the park. Or more unsavory than the usual drug dealers and hookers. And Carissa, monitoring the police calls, had picked it up. I didn't want to be here when the cops arrived.

On the other hand, I didn't want to be riding with the Predators if they were stopped. Or have a picture show up in the paper with me on the back of a known felon's chopped trike. Talk about associating with convicted felons.

"No, thanks," I said. "I'll walk."

"Okay." He gunned the engine and lifted his feet to the rests. "But we ain't done here. I'm gonna get to the bottom of this. And somebody's gonna pay."

If I could talk to Kelly, maybe we could straighten this out some. Or at least maybe I could find out how come she wouldn't come out and talk to me about it.

"How's Kelly doing?" I hollered over the roar of the bikes. "Where is she now?"

"Okay," he shouted back. "But they've decided she's got to go get some physical rehab for a little while."

"Her shoulder?"

"Yeah."

"Where are the kids?"

"With somebody called Aunt Louise. Or a name like that."

They roared off.

I'd met Aunt Louise. She was the older sister or aunt or something of Kelly's ex. The kids would be okay with her. A lot better than with their father, who drank, or with Old Buckles and his buddies. Or in foster care.

I'd spent much of my childhood in foster care. I knew there were some really good foster families out there—I'd spent some time with the Colemans, a deeply religious couple who were not demonstrative but who cared and gave me a solid home while I was there—but they weren't the norm. I wouldn't wish the uncertainty and fear that went with emergency foster care on anybody, much less kids I really liked. Carissa was busy snapping pictures of the departing bikers. Her fur-trimmed suede coat hung open, revealing a tiny scrap of sparkly red fabric I supposed must have been a dress.

The sirens were just down the street. Time for me to make myself scarce. I headed toward the sidewalk that ran past the front of the park, hoping to cross the tracks and dodge down an alley or something.

"Oh, Jesse, can I talk to you?" Carissa called.

Damn. Of course she recognized me.

If she hadn't known me right away, my jacket with its red and black buffalo plaid was a dead giveaway. One of these days I'd have to save up a little money and get myself down to the Goodwill thrift shop and find another one, something less conspicuous.

I debated turning and going the other way back through the park, although I suspected I'd end up against the chain-link fence that surrounded the open area on three sides. I could always climb it. But I wasn't fast enough. She hurried across the sidewalk toward me and grabbed the front of my jacket. I didn't understand how anyone could have moved so fast on those spike heels, but she'd done it.

If I wanted to continue on my way, I'd have had to pry her fingers with the long scarlet nails off my jacket and shove her aside. I stopped.

Smiling, she flipped her hair back. She smelled amazing. "I'm so glad I found you," she said. "You left so fast yesterday! I had to throw out all those breakfast burritos."

That *had* been a loss. But getting away from her was well worth it.

"Why don't we go out to breakfast somewhere now?" she cooed.

"No way." Did she really think I was going to let myself get caught up in a situation like that twice?

"Expense account again," She said, and stuck the tip of her tongue out between her bright pink lips.

I reached up to loosen her grip on my jacket, but she smiled and leaned in close to me.

A patrol car, the source of the siren, pulled up at the curb, and the window rolled down. "What's going on here?" the cop demanded.

"Oooo, officer." Carissa turned to focus her simpering charm on him instead of me. "No problems! We were just talking."

Her charm wasn't working. "Yeah? I got a report of some loud motorcycles in the park."

"There *were* some," Carissa agreed. "But they're gone."

I winced as I realized what this must look like to the two cops in the car. Carissa was dressed like a classy hooker. I was in my oil and grime streaked work clothes. I probably looked like a john. If Carissa wasn't going to be too fussy about who she accepted as a client.

The cop who'd been driving got out of the car and sized us up. He looked like he was coming to exactly the conclusion I was afraid he would.

"What are you doing here?" he asked her. "It's a little early in the morning for a working girl to be out."

"That's not true," Carissa said, tossing her head. "I don't have set hours. I work whenever I need to."

Inwardly, I cringed. Carissa apparently had no idea what he was getting at.

"We were just leaving, officer," I said, desperate to have him stop before he arrested both of us for solicitation. "Just having a little discussion. We were gonna continue it over breakfast."

She beamed up at me. "Yes. We're going to the coffee shop up the street."

"Lover's quarrel?" he asked, his hand resting on his holster.

"Not really," I said. "We don't know each other that well."

The cop smirked. "That's no surprise."

I winced. I'd said exactly the wrong thing.

"Got some ID?" he asked.

I pulled out my wallet and handed him my work ID, which had a picture. "Don't got a driver's license," I said. I did also have my old prison ID, but I wasn't about to bring that out if I didn't have to.

Carissa got an indignant look on her carefully made up face. "Why do you need to see identification?" she demanded.

How could she be so clueless? "Just give it to him, Carissa," I said, hoping she'd cooperate.

"Well." She flipped her hair and dug into her purse, coming up with her wallet. She took two cards out and handed them over. "That one's my driver's license," she said. "And the other's my press card."

The cop raised his eyebrows but took the cards. He handed the cards through the car window to his partner, who had remained in the passenger seat. "You know the guys with the motorcycles?" he asked.

"Some of them," I conceded.

"What did they want?"

"Just wanted to know if I'd seen one of their buddies."

"Yeah? Not trying to sell you some meth or something?"

"No, sir."

"Hey, Barry, come see this," the partner in the car called, opening the door and stepping out. He unsnapped his holster and kept his eyes on me.

"What?" Barry bent down to look at the screen of the computer mounted on the dashboard. He straightened up and looked back at me. "You who I think you are?" he asked.

"Yes, sir. Probably."

"You know your name's come up at a lot of pre-shift briefings?"

I had no good answer to that, so I didn't say anything. But I wasn't particularly surprised.

"Put your hands on top of your head and interlace your fingers," he said.

Still clutching my wallet, I did so.

"What do you think you're doing?" Carissa demanded.

"Let him be," I said to her. "He's just doing his job."

Barry said, "Listen to him. He's right." He reached up and put one hand over mine. To me, he said, "You got anything on you I should know about?"

"No, sir."

"Nothing that's gonna stick me or hurt me?"

"No."

He quickly frisked me, running his hand under my jacket and over my pants. He patted my pockets but didn't remove the keychain. He took the wallet from my hand and looked in it.

"I know what rights we citizens have," Carissa said. "You can search him for weapons, but you need a warrant or probable cause to look in his wallet."

"It's *okay*, Carissa," I said. "I'm on parole. He don't need no reason to search me."

She crossed her thin arms over her narrow chest and sniffed.

"I take it this man isn't coercing you to be with him, ma'am?" Barry said.

"Of course not. I can take care of myself."

"And that press ID is valid?"

She glared. "Definitely. I work for the *Rothsburg Register*. And I'm pursuing a story right now."

"Okay. I just hope you'll be careful, ma'am. Some of these criminal types can be unpredictable. And dangerous."

"You don't have to worry about *me*. But if you don't stop this nonsense you might have to worry about yourselves."

She was going to piss them off, and I'd be the one who suffered the consequences. I said, "Carissa. Shut up."

She spun toward me, an expression on her face I couldn't figure out. Her eyes were half-closed, and her mouth was open. She looked at me, and her tongue traced a circle over her lips.

The radio in the car crackled.

"We done here?" the other cop asked Barry, handing him my wallet and the IDs and moving to get back into the car. "We got an urgent call."

"I guess." Barry glanced down at the cards. "You can put your hands down," he said to me.

Slowly I lowered my hands to my sides. Barry handed the IDs and the wallet, to Carissa. "Here you go."

She took them, glared at him, and handed me my things.

The cops both got into the car, and it tore away, the siren winding up again.

Carissa tossed her head, grabbed me by the elbow and said, "Come on. We're getting breakfast."

I let her lead me away.

We walked down the street past her car and over two blocks, stopping at a trendy little coffee shop near the city hall complex. Office workers were lined up for their morning fix of legal but addictive caffeine. Carissa, still hanging onto my elbow, dragged me past the waiting line and into the back where hanging ferns were hung among mostly empty, dark wooden tables. She steered me to the back and plunked her purse on a chair beside her. She swept the coat off and laid it on top of the purse. The bit of sparkly red fabric *was* a dress of sorts. Since she was so skinny, it managed to hide all the essentials, above and below. I had a feeling a paper napkin could have done just as adequate a job.

"Take off your jacket," she said. "I'll go up and order for us."

I stood there hesitating.

"You're not going to run off on me right away again, are you?"

I probably would have if I were smart. Slipping the jacket off, I said, "I guess not. At least not right away." I sat down and looked at the ferns hanging from the ceiling and the papers with splotches of random color all over them hung on the walls. They were in frames, so I guess they were pictures. Each one had a little price tag in the corner. $150. $200. $500. Must have been some kind of abstract artwork.

Who would spend the best part of a week's wages for any of *that*?

Carissa came back carrying two huge steaming cups of coffee. "I ordered us strawberry crepes," she said and giggled. "I shouldn't really be eating anything with that many calories, especially this early in the morning, but I figured you've been working all night so it would be okay for you. And it sounded so good, I couldn't resist for myself."

Hard to believe anyone as skinny as she was would be worried about getting too many calories. I wasn't entirely sure what crepes were, but I was hungry, and I thought I'd like strawberries. I hadn't had any all those years in prison, and they were too expensive to even think about getting when I went food shopping.

Putting a cup in front of me, she slipped into the seat across the small table. There was hardly enough room for both of our legs under there. I tried to move mine to the side, but hers still rubbed against them.

"So." She tilted her chin down and gave me a sideways smile. "Are you a member of that motorcycle gang?"

The coffee had so much other stuff in it—milk and whipped cream on top—that it was only lukewarm. I took a big swallow and said, "No, ma'am. They're trouble. I try to keep my distance from folks like that."

"Yet you were in the park with them this morning."

"Yeah." I took another drink. "That one guy on the trike, Old Buckles, he's Kelly's dad. We were talking about how she was doing." Not the entire truth, but close enough.

She smirked. "Kelly's dad is a biker? We're talking the Kelly who was raped?"

If I'd realized she didn't know that, I wouldn't have mentioned it. Too late now. I just said, "Yeah."

"And you didn't know him before you started seeing Kelly?"

"No. I knew him first. We were locked up in the same medium security prison for a while."

"So you know him from prison?"

"Kind of. I mean, we weren't close or nothing. But he worked as a commissary clerk, and pretty much everybody had to deal with him at one time or another."

"Were you a member of the gang *before* you got locked up?"

My criminal background was an easily accessible public record. *Weren't reporters supposed to do background research when they were doing a feature story? By now, this wasn't a spur-of-the-moment thing—she'd had plenty of time to look it up.* "I was *sixteen* when I got locked up. And I was living in Baltimore City. No, I wasn't hanging with a bike club based in Rothsburg at that point. If they were even active twenty years ago."

"So you hooked up with them after you were released from prison?"

I pushed my chair back and reached for my jacket. "If you ain't gonna believe what I say, I'm sure as hell not gonna stay here and possibly incriminate myself trying to explain."

She put her hand on my arm. "Wait. I'm sorry. Sometimes I just push too hard. That's kind of a reporter's job, you know."

I didn't know, and I was pretty sure that any reporter who was this clumsy about it wouldn't get too far. But I dropped the jacket back on the chair.

She pulled that simpering smile again and leaned across the table, dropping her chest and throwing back her shoulders so I could see down the front of her dress. I tried to tell myself that there really wasn't much to see, but I was getting a new understanding of the expression "moth to the flame."

She said, "I'd like to do a feature story on that gang. What's their name—the Preyers?"

Which sounded so much like it might be a fanatical religious group called the Prayers that I had to laugh. It broke the spell. "The Predators," I said.

"So how would I go about getting closer to the group so I could find out what's going on with them?"

"Not a good idea."

She pouted. "Why not?"

"If you hang around them, they're gonna expect things from you."

"What kinds of things?"

May as well be bluntly honest. "Sex."

She sat up straighter. "Sex."

"Yeah."

"What's so bad about that?"

That struck me as an interesting way to look at it. "For one thing, it wouldn't be on your terms."

"What do you mean, 'not on my terms'?"

"If they figure you've come to party and everybody gets going, no-body's gonna *ask* you if you want to go along with whatever they want to do."

"I'm a big girl. I can take care of myself."

"You're not gonna have much choice in who's your partner. Or part-ners."

Her eyes opened wide. Her voice breathy, she said, "Group sex?"

I hadn't spent all that time in prison with various cell buddies without hearing all the gory details of how biker parties usually went. "Maybe. Or one at a time, but a lot of them. And it's gonna be rougher than any-thing you're used to."

She sniffed. "How do *you* know what kind of sex I'm used to?"

I had to admit she had me there. "I don't. But you don't look like the type to go for that type of stuff."

"I'll have you know I like 'bad boys.'"

Not looking at her, I nodded.

She leaned close. "You want to find out what kind of sex I'm used to?"

Alarmed, I sat up straight. "No, ma'am." I had enough problems in my life.

A waitress arrived with two plates of crepes, placing them on the table between us. Good timing. The waitress looked too harried to have caught our conversation.

A crepe seemed to be some kind of a thin flat pancake which was rolled around a filling of strawberries and smothered in whipped cream. I took a taste. Delicious.

Carissa lifted a forkful of whipped cream, but instead of opening her mouth and eating it, she flicked out her tongue and caressed the cream.

I concentrated on my own breakfast.

"I understand the gang has a clubhouse out in the hills somewhere," she said.

"Yeah."

"Will you take me out there?"

She just didn't believe me. "I've never been there. And I'm not plan-ning to go."

"This is important to me." She reached for my hand. "I *really* want to do a feature story. Maybe get out to a party there. It could be a turning point in my career."

A turning point in her life, I thought. And not in a good way. She'd lose some of her naiveté pretty quickly if she got out there during a party. It might change her thinking about a lot of things. I said, "No."

She pulled that pouting number and tossed her hair back.

"Look." I pushed my now empty plate to the side and took the coffee cup. "I appreciate you buying me breakfast and all. But you can't get involved with the Predators to do a story. You're either a member, or it's not safe. Even then, it might not be safe."

"How do I get to be a member?"

This wasn't working at all. "Only way a woman can get to be a member is to hook up with one of the men. Then it would be hard to get out of it. So just forget it. Find something else to do a feature story about."

"Like what?"

"I dunno. Must be lots of stuff. But messing around with the Predators is *not* a good idea."

"You mess with them."

"Not if I can help it." And if it wasn't for Kelly, I wouldn't mess with them at all. "And I got to be going." I took the last swallow of coffee.

She tilted her head and smiled up at me. "Where are you going?"

"Home. I worked all night. I got to get some sleep."

"Can I come with you?"

I almost choked on the coffee. Was she as hot to trot as she made out? Or would she lead me on and then pull out at the last minute? Or follow through, think better of it, and claim she'd been raped?

She was not the kind of complication I needed in my life right now. Of course I was interested—what man wouldn't be?—but up until now, casual sex wasn't part of my life. And I had a feeling that, even if I decided to go in that direction, Carissa would be a poor choice to start with.

Trying to sort out what was going on with Kelly was more than enough.

"No." I got to my feet.

She made a face and stuck out her tongue.

I grabbed my jacket and left.

CHAPTER 8

I had to pass the public library on my way home and decided to check today's edition of the *Rothsburg Register* to see if Carissa had written any more articles that included me. Or taken any more pictures I wasn't aware of.

As I came through the front door, Mandy Sterling, the clerk who worked at the circulation desk greeted me.

Mandy had been the person who had accepted my prison ID and copy of the lease on my apartment as adequate when I'd first applied for a library card. And she hadn't acted like there was anything unusual about someone having a prison ID. I would be eternally grateful to her for that.

No one was at the desk to check out anything, and Mandy stood, a book in her hand, staring out the window and frowning. I went up to say hello. She wore a plain pullover sweater and a cardigan of the sort my former foster mother would have called "a twin set." Only Mandy's looked soft and luxurious, like it was made of cashmere. Diamonds mounted in platinum sparkled at her earlobes and a heavy matching pendant hung from her neck. Or maybe, for all I could tell, they were cubic zirconium in steel. On her, though, probably not.

Her parents had died, I remembered, and she was an only child, so she had inherited a house and lots of other nice things. She probably didn't need to work, but I knew she didn't have much of a social life, and the job was important to her.

As someone who had worked in a prison laundry for years for a dollar a day, I understood how important it could be to have a structured routine in life that required attendance at work on a daily basis, even if the money wasn't important. She probably figured working was much better than being stuck home all day. I thought working for a dollar a day was better than being stuck in a cell all day.

Of course, the dollar a day had been important to me. Some of the other inmates had people out on the street who sent them money orders for their commissary accounts, but I didn't know anybody who cared that much about me. I didn't get any mail at all, much less money orders. So the only money I had was what the laundry job paid.

"How've you been?" I asked.

Mandy frowned. "I've been better. It's been a bad day."

There probably wasn't much I could do, but I tried to sympathize. "What happened?"

"Somebody stole my car."

I winced. "From out of your garage?" I asked.

"No. I guess I should have put it in the garage, but I had groceries to bring in, and I'd left it out in the driveway. When I went out to go to work, it was gone."

If I'd gone out and found my ride missing, I'd be plenty pissed. Of course, that was assuming I ever got a car.

"I had to walk to work," Mandy continued. "And now I have to go through all this nonsense with the police and the insurance company."

A chilling thought occurred to me. "It wasn't a silver Lexus by any chance, was it?"

"No. It was a Mercedes 350 coupe. Bright red." Tears pooled in her eyes. "I *loved* that car. And I'd just had it a few years. It was almost new!"

"Maybe somebody just took it for a joyride," I said. "And if it's recovered, it might be fine."

"The police said they'd look, but they said there'd been a lot of car thefts lately. Especially nice, newer model ones. They took a report, but they said if it didn't have a LoJack or something, I'd probably never see it again."

"So what did you do?"

"I called the insurance company."

That made sense.

A few people came up to the desk with books to check out. I nodded to Mandy and went to the reading room where they kept recent newspapers and magazines. The last few days' copies of the *Rothsburg Register* were stacked on a round table in front of a comfy couch and a few chairs. I plopped down in one of the chairs and sorted through the pile of newspapers, pulling out the latest one.

Sure enough, there was the beginning of an article with Carissa's byline on the front page, continued further back in the paper. And it had a picture, but it was of Carissa. I read the first few paragraphs, then flipped to the rest of it. It was mostly about how Carissa Daniles had just graduated from college and was a new reporter with the paper. For now, she was assigned to the police and court beat, and would be writing feature articles about unsavory happenings in the area.

Fine by me, as long as those articles didn't feature *me*.

"Jesse!"

I looked up. A little girl was flying across the reading room toward me. I barely had enough time to get my arms up to catch her as she landed on me.

Brianna, Kelly's six-year-old daughter. She buried her face in my chest, sobbing.

Chris, her older brother, was right behind her. "Jesse, what are you doing here?" he asked.

"Reading," I said. "People come to the library to do lots of things, but reading is one of them."

"I like to come use the computer," he told me.

He was only eight, but he was light-years ahead of me on that score. I'd never used a computer.

Brianna settled down in my lap, her face still pressed against my shirt. Since I hadn't taken a shower after work, I was sure I smelled of oil and sweat, but she didn't seem to mind. Her mother probably smelled that way after work sometimes, too.

"Why aren't you guys in school?" I asked.

"No school today. Have you seen our mom?"

I wasn't going to lie to the kids, but I didn't have to tell them the whole truth. "Yeah, I saw her at the hospital. She was pretty tired, but she was getting better."

Chris's face twisted. "I wish she'd come home."

My chest tightened. What with their parents' divorce and all the crap that lead up to it, things hadn't been easy for them. And now this. "She will as soon as she can. Who's taking care of you now?"

He nodded toward a petite, elderly woman who was leaning on a cane, making her way toward us. "Aunt Louise."

I'd met Aunt Louise, who I thought was their father's aunt, and I knew she would take good care of them. But she was awfully old for the responsibility. And she was taking care of her *own* mother, too, who, if I remembered right, was bedridden.

"Are you checking any books out?" I asked.

"Yeah. We have to go to the dentist with Aunt Louise," Chris said. "And we're getting books to read while we wait for her. We have to be very good, and then she might take us for a hot dog."

Aunt Louise came to a stop next to us and nodded. The side of her face was swollen. "I have a toothache," she said. "The dentist said he could fit me in, but I don't have anyone to leave the children with. Mother's not in any shape to look after them, and Fred hasn't shown up lately."

Fred was Kelly's ex, the children's father. He was the one who was supposed to be taking responsibility for the kids. They were much better off with Aunt Louise.

I sat up a little straighter, shifting Brianna's weight in my lap. Should I offer to pitch in? Kelly might not be happy about it, but she wasn't here. Up until now, she'd encouraged me to spend time with them. I hadn't done anything that should change that. And this might be the last chance I got to spend any time with the kids. A cold lump formed in my stomach at that thought. I really liked being with the kids.

"Do you want me to keep an eye on them while you're at the dentist?" I asked.

Aunt Louise looked thoughtful. She knew Kelly let me stay at the house sometimes, but Fred probably knew all about my conviction and being on parole and told her about it. He was trying to get custody away from Kelly, which was problematic, since he was an alcoholic and the kids had been in the car one night when he'd been in an accident. He'd picked up a DUI for that, but it hadn't stopped the court from ordering that he be permitted to take the kids for visitation.

Of course, Kelly had an alcohol problem, too, although I didn't think it was as bad as his. And it was a good thing there'd been somewhere for the kids to go with Kelly in the hospital. I knew from my own childhood experience how scary and disruptive it could be to suddenly end up in an emergency foster home. I was glad these kids didn't have to go through that.

"The dentist is just down the street," Aunt Louise said. "What would you do with the children if I left them with you?"

"We could stay here in the library," I said. "Read books or use the computers. I don't imagine you'd be gone much more than an hour or two, do you?"

"I hope not. You'll be sure to stay in the library? Not take them anywhere else?"

"Yes, ma'am. We'll stay in the library." I tried to look reliable, but I'm not sure I was successful.

She made up her mind. "All right. I'll be back as soon as I can be. You children behave and don't make noise. It's a *library*."

"We'll go into the children's section," I said.

Aunt Louise nodded and turned to leave.

"Jesse," Chris said.

"Yes?"

"Do you know if the Goddess and the kittens are okay? Some of PopPop's friends weren't being nice to them."

The Goddess was the cat I'd found and Kelly had taken in. She was a quiet cat who'd pretty much stay to herself, but some of the bikers were likely to kick any animal that got in their way. The Goddess might just corral the kittens down in the basement or something and hide from people. I hoped so.

"She's probably fine," I said with more assurance than I felt. "She'd keep her kittens out of the way of people who didn't like cats. And your mom had that great big bag of cat food in the kitchen, so even if nobody remembered to feed them, they'd knock that over and eat from the spilled food."

She'd knocked it over a few times when I'd been over there and she didn't think we'd fed her quickly enough. I couldn't imagine any of the bikers bothering to clean up spilled cat food.

Holding Brianna, who still had her face buried in my shirt, I stood up and took Chris's hand. He was too old to wander away or anything, so he didn't *need* me to hold his hand. But I could remember times when I was a scared kid and would have been grateful for a strong, supporting hand to hold, even if just for a few minutes.

A number of preschoolers and their mothers gathered around in the children's room of the library for the daily story times. A bunch of older kids were there, too. Apparently there was no school today—otherwise Aunt Louise would have taken Brianna and Chris, and not had to worry about them while she was at the dentist. I wasn't sure why—was this a minor holiday of some sort? Didn't Presidents Day or something come around now?

We got a fair number of stares as we came in. I was still in my dirty work clothes, in need of a shave, and my face was still bruised. I was aware that both of the kids looked as miserable as they felt. I wished I'd had a chance to take a shower and change. I didn't have many clothes, but not all of them were *this* grungy.

The computers were all in use. Chris went to the desk and signed up for a session, but he'd have to wait his turn. Brianna got some books for me to read to her. She loved to have books read to her, but I knew Kelly struggled with reading and didn't do it much. Brianna seemed to have inherited the same problem, but Kelly refused to have her tested for special education, which would have given her some extra help in reading in school.

We settled into a couch in a corner where we couldn't be seen very well and where we were out of the way of all the hustle. Chris brought a book for me to read, too. They sat on either side of me, both snuggling in against me. They needed as much comforting physical contact as they could get.

Truth be told, so did I.

I tried to just savor the moment and put out of my mind the fact that Kelly would have been livid if she could have seen us.

When Chris got called for his time on the computer a few minutes later, Brianna climbed into my lap and leaned back against me. She stuck her fingers in her mouth and looked at the pictures in the book as I read the story.

We were just finishing *Horton Hatches a Who*—Brianna usually laughs out loud at the rhymes, but today she just stared intently—when someone came around the corner of the shelving that shielded our little hideaway.

Two uniformed police officers, a man and a woman.

My throat closed up, and I stopped breathing. Brianna shrunk back against my chest. Chris abandoned his computer and came dashing to us.

"Just want to ask you a few questions," the man said, his hand resting on his holster. "Stand up."

Please don't pull out a weapon here, I thought, but I didn't say anything to him. To Brianna, I said, "I have to stand up now, honey, so you'll have to get off my lap."

She didn't move. I eased her into the seat next to me and stood. Chris stood there blankly. I said, "Can you sit next to her, please?"

"Why are they bothering you, Jesse?" Chris asked, a hitch in his voice. "They tell us in school policemen are supposed to be our friends, but sometimes they *hurt* you."

"Policemen *are* your friends," I said. "Remember the time they gave you and Brianna teddy bears? And they don't want to hurt people, but sometimes there's an accident or something."

The woman cop waved the librarian over. "We don't want to upset everyone if we can handle this quietly. Is there an office or someplace we could take him to for a few minutes?"

The librarian nodded toward her office, which had a big glass window opening into the children's room. "You could use that office. There is a shade you could draw."

"Okay. Can you stay with these kids for a few minutes?"

Motherly concern clouded her chubby face. "I suppose."

I stood up and looked questioningly at the male cop. "Cuffs?"

"Not in front of the kids if we can help it," he said. "You gonna be compliant with my orders?"

"Yeah."

He took a firm hold on my arm and propelled me ahead of him toward the office.

"Where are you taking Jesse?" Brianna wailed. "He's my mommy's boyfriend."

"Hush, Brianna," I said. "This is a library. We're supposed to be quiet. I'll be back in a few minutes." I looked at the female cop's narrowed eyes. "Or Aunt Louise will come. You'll be fine."

Which was more than I could say for me.

We got into the office, and the female cop drew the shade, then closed the door and stood in front of it. She unsnapped her holster and rested her hand on the butt of her service gun.

"I'd just as soon we handle this without creating a fuss with all the kids in here," her partner said, letting go of my arm. "I'm gonna search you for weapons. Face the back wall. Put your hands on your head and interlace your fingers."

He did a quick pat down, but didn't remove the wallet and keychain. I had nothing else in my pockets.

"Okay," he said. "I take it you're not the kids' father."

"No, sir."

"You're their mother's boyfriend?"

Tricky question. "Sometimes."

"And where is the mother?"

"She was in the hospital. She might still be."

"And how come you're with the kids? You taking care of them until their mother gets back?"

I knew the truth was going to sound far-fetched, but it was all I had to give them. "No. They're staying with their aunt. But she had a dentist appointment, and she needed somebody to keep an eye on them for a little while."

The cop looked doubtful. "So she called *you* to come take care of them?"

"No. She was in here getting them books to read in the dentist's waiting room, and I ran into her. I offered to keep an eye on them."

"We're aware of who you are, you know," he said.

"I figured."

"The librarian thought you and the kids looked a little off when you came in. They watch for things like that. Then you took them into the back corner. She called the people who work in the adult department, and one of them knew your name."

Mandy.

"Then she called us, and after we looked you up, we decide to come in and check out the situation."

No surprise there.

Someone knocked on the door. The female cop went over and opened it. I glanced over my shoulder. The librarian stood there. She stared at me, still with my back to the cops and my hands on my head.

"The children's aunt is here," she said. "She seems a little unstable on her feet."

"Send her in."

Glancing over my shoulder, I saw Aunt Louise totter into the office, clutching her cane.

"Keep facing the wall," the cop told me.

I snapped my head back around.

"May I sit down?" Aunt Louise asked. "I've just come from the dentist. He wanted me to stay a little while longer until I felt stronger, but I had to get back to see how the children were doing."

I could hear someone pull a chair out for her.

"Did you leave the kids with this man?" the female cop asked.

"With Jesse? Yes, I did. And Chris—he's the older child—told me nothing much happened, that he was just reading stories to them when you officers arrived. He's afraid that you are going to hurt Jesse. Or take him to jail."

Distinct possibility, that. Especially the jail part.

The cop asked, "Do you know who this person is?"

"I know he's a..." she paused, "'friend' of the children's mother's. I know she trusts the children with him."

"Do you know that he's a convict out on parole?"

"I knew he's just been released from prison a little while ago. I don't know what he was convicted of. I sincerely hope you're not going to tell me that it's child molestation."

"No. But it's murder."

"Of a child?"

"No."

"Then what's the problem? Did you find a weapon or drugs on him? I mean, of course it would have been better if he had never killed anyone, but I can't see it makes him an unfit person to stay for a little while with children who know him and like him. And in a public place."

I could have kissed Aunt Louise. Although that might have gotten both of us shot if I put my hands down and moved to do that.

"Okay," the male cop said to me. "You can put your hands down and turn around."

I did so. The two cops glanced at each other.

Aunt Louise sat in a desk chair, looking even more fatigued than she had before. Her face was still swollen, and she must have had Novocain shots since her eyelid and mouth drooped on that side.

No one said anything for a few seconds.

"Are we done here?" Aunt Louise asked. "I'm not feeling all that well, and the children haven't had their lunch yet. I'd like to take them to get something to eat, then go home so I can lie down."

The male cop nodded. "You can get the children and go."

Aunt Louise struggled to her feet and leaned on her cane. She looked at me. "Jesse? Are you coming to lunch with us? I could really use the help with the children."

Trying not to show my amazement, I said, "Yes, ma'am," and stepped past the cops. No one grabbed me or told me to stop, so I held the door open for Aunt Louise as she hobbled out into the children's room and followed her over to the corner where the kids and I had been sitting.

The kids were still there, and the librarian was trying to get them interested in a book she held. They weren't paying attention.

When she saw me, Brianna sprang up and grabbed my leg. Chris took my hand.

"Jesse," he said. "I thought they were going to *do* something to do. Or take you away."

I smiled down at him. "See. It was just a misunderstanding that we got sorted out. I *told* you police officers were your friends."

Aunt Louise supported herself unsteadily with her cane. "Were you children well-behaved like you promised?" she asked.

They nodded.

"Good. Then we're all going to Texas Hot Weiner for lunch."

"Jesse, too?" Chris asked.

"Jesse, too."

I took each kid by the hand, and we followed Aunt Louise out of the library.

CHAPTER 9

Texas Hot Weiner was doing a steady lunch hour business, but we managed to snag a booth along the wall. I helped Aunt Louise ease her bulk into the seat and deposited the kids across from her. "What does everybody want?" I asked, mentally calculating how much money I had as I reached for my wallet. This might be the last chance I had to treat the kids. I'd worry later about what I'd have to do without to pay for it.

"Don't be silly," Aunt Louise said, opening her purse and extracting a twenty dollar bill. "I was planning to cover this."

I turned my wallet over in my hand. "But..."

Aunt Louise glared at me. "I said, *I'm* paying."

I could see why nobody argued much with Aunt Louise. I said, "Yes, ma'am," and took the twenty.

"A chili dog," Chris said.

"And root beer," Brianna added.

"And don't you forget to get yourself lunch, too," Aunt Louise said. "Just being able to sit here while you do the running back and forth is a Godsend."

I brought back chili dogs, root beer, and a big order of fries.

Aunt Louise said her mouth didn't feel good enough to eat a chili dog, so she gave hers to me.

After lunch, we went out to Aunt Louise's car.

Seeing how unsteady she still seemed, I asked. "Do you feel well enough to drive?" Since I didn't have a driver's license, I wasn't sure what I could do about it if she'd said no, but she said she felt well enough to drive the short distance home.

I planted a kiss on each kid's forehead and ruffled their brown hair before they got in the car. The lump in my throat made it hard to tell them goodbye. This might very well be the last time I saw them. I tried to tell myself that I hadn't known them for that long, so how could they mean much to me anyhow? But I knew I was lying to myself. Even worse was the fear that they'd think I'd abandoned them.

I went to my apartment and knew I should try to get some rest before work. But I doubted I could sleep, so instead of going to bed, I collected my laundry. I didn't have many clothes, and they got dirty fast at work. If

I tried to go a whole week between trips to the Laundromat, I ran out of clean clothes and ended up going to work in clothes already grimy from a previous shift.

Tuesdays weren't a busy time at the Laundromat.

I lugged along a bottle of detergent and one of fabric softener.

When I'd worked in the prison laundry, the guy who trained me on the equipment had run a commercial laundry before he got locked up, and he spoke longingly of the scent of freshly washed sheets when fabric softener was added to the final rinse. Curious, I'd splurged on a bottle the first time I bought detergent. And I was hooked. After years of the prison smells of unwashed bodies, urine, and disinfectant, I could imagine no greater luxury than falling asleep in my own bed, snuggled into just-washed sheets that carried the scent of fabric softener.

Unless of course it was falling asleep in *Kelly's* bed, where the aroma of the sheets would mingle with Kelly's earthy scent.

I'd better stop thinking like that. Whatever had happened to Kelly, she didn't want to see me. Maybe she even believed the nonsense about me and Razorback agreeing to trade women. And if she believed it, it didn't matter whether it was true or not.

The biggest hurt was that Kelly thought I could do something like. She must not trust me at all. Although why should she?

I separated out my grease-covered work clothes and dumped them in one machine. I knew all about separating the whites from the colors, but I didn't care if my underwear came out the color of my towels, so I stuffed everything else together in another machine.

Doing the laundry was expensive. Every week when I cashed my paycheck, I got a ten dollar roll of quarters for laundry. I tried to get by on that for the week. My work clothes had too much oil and grime to put in with anything else, so I did them in a separate load. Since a quarter only bought seven minutes of dryer time, sometimes I ended up taking some of the stuff home damp and hanging it around the apartment to dry.

But not the sheets. I always made sure they were completely dry.

The machines whirled to life. I wandered over to read the ads posted on the bulletin board. Sometimes I thought maybe I could pick up a few extra bucks answering a few of them and doing some extra work during the day or on weekends. But almost everybody wanted references. I didn't think my background was going to exactly encourage anyone to hire me.

In the mid-morning stillness, I heard a vehicle pull up to the curb. Somebody else coming in to do laundry. I liked to have the place to myself, but it was a public facility.

The door burst open, and a huge bundle of laundry hit the floor, bursting open and exploding clothes all over. A black lacy bra sprang up and hung itself on the edge of a folding table.

"Oh, shit," a female voice exclaimed.

I turned to look, and recognized Li'l Mama.

No reason I could think of that she'd recognize me. Unless someone had pointed me out to her at some point. So I didn't say anything.

She stood in the doorway, her makeup smeared and her hands on her hips, glaring at the clothes tumbled all over the floor. The mountain was high and wide enough that she couldn't get into the Laundromat without stepping on the clothes.

I wasn't doing much, so I pulled a cart over and started scooping the clothes off the floor and putting them in the cart. She looked at me and shook her head. "Thanks, mister," she said and bent down to clear a path so she could come grab another cart.

Apparently she didn't know who I was. *Fine by me.*

I continued to shovel clothes into the cart. Socks. More bras. A rather alarming pair of panties in a shiny pink fabric that seemed to be missing the crotch. A matching and equally alarming bra that had holes where the cups should be.

Then men's clothes. Blue jeans that smelled of motor oil and exhaust. T-shirts with sweat stains under the armpits. Heavy socks and boxers. Tighty whities.

How many people was she doing laundry for?

The cart was full. I just picked up bunches of clothes from the floor and piled them on a folding table.

The whole mess had a funky aura, but I'd certainly handled worse in the prison laundry, especially from the infirmary. That laundry was often drenched in blood and puke and shit and piss.

Li'l Mama finally put the last bit on the table and looked at it in disgust. "I lost," she said.

I had no idea what she was talking about. "What?"

"We drew to see who had to go do everybody's laundry. I lost."

"Oh." That explained the sheer volume of laundry.

"At least I didn't have to chip in," she said, dumping a pile of coins and dollar bills on another table. "I told them if I had to wash all this crap, they could pony up for it."

Seemed fair to me. I checked the machines with my wash. Time to add fabric softener.

She stared at me in fascination as I measured out capfuls and dumped them in. "What does that do?"

"Makes it smell nice."

"Really? You care how your clothes smell?"

I shrugged. "More the sheets. But yeah, I'd just as soon my clothes smelled okay when I get done with washing them. They get funky smelling soon enough."

She shrugged and started sorting out the mountain, putting the delicate undies in one machine, the sturdy underwear in another, and the blue jeans in third. She still had piles of shirts and towels to go.

Grabbing a free real estate catalog from a pile on the front windowsill, I sat down and started flipping through the pages. Houses for sale. Hundreds of thousands of dollars. Even little shacky-looking houses were in the six digit category. *How could anyone ever afford to buy a house?*

No wonder Kelly was trying so hard to hang onto the house she and her ex had bought when they were married. If she lost it, she'd never be able to afford another one.

Kelly. The familiar pang shot through my gut. Maybe Li'l Mama had been to see her, or talked to somebody who had. She had a much better chance of finding out something than I did. *Would she tell me if I asked?*

She might. But I'd have to tell her who I was if I wanted her to even consider talking to me. She'd go back and tell everybody all about it, maybe spread some more rumors. And I might not even find out anything useful.

I watched as she crammed clothes in the washing machines. Way more than the instructions said. She inserted quarters into the slots and dumped in detergent without measuring it. Then she kicked off her boots and sank down in a chair a near me.

What did I really have to lose if I asked about Kelly?

I got up to switch my clothes to the dryers and sat back down again. Licking my lips, I said, "You hear how Kelly's doing?"

She sat up straight and stared at me. "What's it to you?"

I shrugged. "Just wondered, is all."

"Who are *you*?"

Maybe I could get away without giving my name. "Just somebody who works with her."

"At that steel factory?"

"Yeah."

She fiddled with her earring, which sported a chain that hung halfway to her shoulder. "You wouldn't be *Jesse* by any chance, would you?"

No point lying. "Yeah."

"Wow. Kelly's pretty mad at you, you know."

I nodded.

"But Black Rose, she's talking you up good."

"Black Rose?" The one Old Buckles thought I'd screwed. He just wasn't sure whether I'd also told Razorback he could have a go at Kelly. She'd also gone with Li'l Mama to see Kelly at the hospital.

"You know. Razorback's old lady."

I nodded. That much I knew. "What's she saying?"

"She's saying if Razorback don't show up again soon, she's gonna hook up with you."

Not if I had anything to do with it. "I don't imagine Razorback thinks too much of that idea. Anybody seen him lately?"

She tilted her head and raised her eyebrows. "You didn't hear?"

"Hear what?"

"He's made himself pretty scarce since everybody's mad at him for what he did to Kelly. And since he's on the sex offender registry, he's in trouble for not reporting a change of address. Old Buckles is gonna give him what for. If he don't get locked up first. They're looking for him."

"I'd heard that. But I didn't think he'd be gone for long. I mean, he's got a business to run and all, don't he?"

Li'l Mama shifted on the seat and made a snorting noise. "Yeah, well. It's mostly Black Rose runs the business. Me and Funky Joe been trying to help her. It's much easier to load the backhoe on the trailer with two people. Joe tries to get to wherever she's working and help her. But he's working that construction job at the bridge site along with most of the guys, so if she's got to move it during the day, she has to do it herself."

"The same place Old Buckles' working?"

"Yeah. Some guy he knows, construction foreman out there, he needed a crew fast and he let Old Buckles bring a whole bunch of the guys for day jobs out there. Sorry state of affairs when the guy who's just out of prison is the one finding jobs for everybody else. And I been trying to take the phone messages and schedule work for her."

"Lots of work now?"

"Yeah, especially out in the neighborhood by that bridge. They put in new sewer mains and everybody's got to hook up. To do that, they need a trench dug."

"So if Razorback doesn't show up, the business'll be okay?"

"Probably. The club'll help out if she needs it. They use a big garage on the property for a clubhouse, so they'd chip in for the mortgage."

"If they got that clubhouse, how come everybody's been spending so much time at Kelly's place in town?" I asked.

She shrugged. "Old Buckles been staying mostly in town. While he was locked up, some of the guys got into some stuff he's not real happy about. So there's a lot going on at the clubhouse right now. He thinks they're maybe keeping a close eye on him since he just got released, and he don't want to call attention to none of it. So he's been keeping away."

"And Razorback's not staying up there now, either?"

"Nope. The cops are looking to lock him up. They came up nosing around, but they didn't have a search warrant, and no probable cause, so they left."

"So where has Razorback gone?"

"Don't nobody know. Black Rose says she's got all his stuff. He didn't even take his chopper."

I'd heard that. And it didn't sound good. The bikers I knew didn't much care if the cops stopped them. In fact, they got a kick out of it and sometimes encouraged it. But I guess not if they were registered sex offenders who were wanted on new rape charges.

"He prob'ly figured it was too noticeable," she continued. "It's bright purple, and he's got it really chromed up. Cops'd pick it right up if he tried to take off on it."

I tried to get her back to my main topic of interest. "So is Kelly gonna be okay?"

"Should be. No broken bones that I know of. But she might have to go to a rehab for her shoulder."

That was bad enough. "No head injury?" I asked.

"Well, a concussion. She was knocked out, which is why somebody called 9-1-1. Thought she might be really hurt."

"When'll she get out of the hospital?"

"Might be at the rehab already. But she's not supposed to go back to work for another week or something."

"That's okay. The whole place is shut down for retooling next week. We all get one of our vacation weeks." Even I would get paid, since I was now off the probationary period and a full-fledged union member.

"Oh. You gonna go to the rehab to see her?"

"I don't think she wants to see me."

"You may be right. She says she ain't never gonna let you touch her again."

I was afraid that might be the truth. Of course if she were raped, she was pretty traumatized. Maybe she wouldn't want sex for a while. If she trusted me, I was sure we could work that out.

But as it was, she didn't trust me. And if she didn't trust me, I didn't see much future for us.

"Black Rose says if she don't take you back, she's missing out on a good thing."

"Exactly what does Black Rose say?"

Li'l Mama leaned toward me and smiled. "Black Rose says you're welcome back in *her* bed anytime."

I shifted uncomfortably in my seat. "I don't know what she's talking about."

She winked. "She *said* you'd be a gentleman about it. Not gonna go bragging and such. And you ain't rough and tumble like most of the guys. They want what they want when they want it and a girl'd just better relax and get what she can out of it. But she says you take your time and make sure the girl's liking it too."

I felt heat rising to my face. I had almost no sexual experience—none with anybody but Kelly—and here was this experienced biker chick telling everybody what my sex life was like. And she may have hit the nail on the head.

She laughed. "Black Rose sure got the better of that deal. She got a good time, and poor Kelly got the crap beat out of her."

"I don't know where Black Rose got that. There was no deal."

"That's what you say now that it's gone bad. You and Black Rose got your jollies, but Kelly wasn't too happy with the arrangement. She said you never even told her, and she hadn't agreed. So she didn't want to follow through. She'd been drinking and Razorback was high, so he got mad and took what he wanted anyhow. He's got a history of that."

I gripped the real estate catalog so hard my hands ached. "He had no right to do that to her."

"It sure did create a real mess. Black Rose says he should have backed off and could have worked it out with you. But she's glad she got hers first. Said getting it on with you was an experience she'd never forget."

I could just imagine the response I'd get if Li'l Mama saw me blush. She'd think it was hilarious and wouldn't stop until she'd told everyone she could. I got up to check my laundry. It wasn't dry yet. My gut churning, I went back and sat down.

Li'l Mama smirked at me and raised one eyebrow. The one with the big gold ring through it. "You know, Funky Joe's my old man. You wanna make some kind of arrangement with him, I got no problem with it. Not after what Black Rose says about you. Maybe drugs or something. Even cash. But I think you'd just better leave Kelly out of it."

"Funky Joe's not real happy with me right now," I said.

"He'll get over it." Li'l Mama tossed her head, reminding me of Carissa. "Men don't tend to sweat how anybody feels about crap like that."

Except maybe for me. I cared about how Kelly felt about me. I cared a lot. I might never be able to figure out what happened to her—to *us*, really, if there'd ever really been an "us" outside of my daydreams—but I definitely cared.

CHAPTER 10

Thursday morning was my regular appointment with Mr. Ramirez, my parole officer. In general, the appointments made me nervous—here was a man who could send me back to prison with his signature on a piece of paper—I sure wasn't looking forward to what he would have to say about what had happened over the last week.

Right after work, I headed over there. As I walked, I tried to figure out some way to put a positive spin on the last week. Or at least not quite such a negative one. I didn't come up with any ideas. Even to me, any way I tried to explain it sounded like I'd gotten mixed up in a lot of stuff I shouldn't have. *Again.*

So far, Mr. Ramirez had been pretty reasonable and even supportive of me. As he put it, he wanted people on parole out working and paying taxes, so he could retire one day and collect his Social Security. But he had a limited tolerance for someone who kept getting in new trouble. Even if I didn't pick up new charges, he still had the power to put me back on house arrest. Or lock me back up for a long time.

Trouble just seemed to find me. I didn't know if it would get better after I'd been out on the street for a while, but right now it seemed like I couldn't keep my nose clean no matter how hard I tried. Belkins and Montgomery weren't much help, but I seemed to be able to manage to find problems all on my own. And now here I was on my way to see my parole officer with no good way to explain away how I'd gotten locked up over the weekend or why I was hanging out with bikers.

The parole office was in the basement of the county building, which also housed the jail, police headquarters, and a courthouse. Convenient enough that the cops often didn't bother to go out and look for a parolee with a retake warrant. All they had to do was ask the receptionist to call upstairs when whoever they wanted showed up for an appointment.

The waiting room was overheated and damp with moisture condensing on the grimy windows set high in the walls. I signed in on the clipboard on the ledge outside the window to the unoccupied receptionist's desk. Then I wiped a seat in the corner dry with my jacket and sat down to wait. At this early hour, the room was empty.

The outer door opened, and someone else came in. He was thin and tall, but he walked hunched over, which made him look shorter than he was. He staggered over to sign in, then lurched over to a chair in the far corner and promptly closed his eyes. I kept a wary eye on him.

"Jesse Damon?" A woman with big hair and a bigger bosom had appeared form down the hallway and picked up the clipboard and called me surprisingly quickly. My heart sank, and I tried to look past her to see if a couple of burly cops with handcuffs were behind her at the window. I didn't see anyone, but they might be trying to remain out of sight. Not a whole hell of a lot I could do about it anyhow. She had a bored expression on her face and was chewing a wad of gum.

I got to my feet and went up to the window. She opened the door next to it and indicated a chair by her desk.

"Got your fee?" she asked.

Of course they'd want their money. "Yes, ma'am." I took out my wallet. The costs of parole supervision took a big chunk out of my not quite adequate paychecks. At least I was no longer on house arrest and paying those fees, too.

She took the money and typed something in on the computer. "Urinalysis fee?" she asked.

"I don't usually have to get tested," I said. Although Mr. Ramirez could change that any time.

"That'd be unusual," she said, but she kept looking. "You're right. I wonder why?"

I wasn't sure that was really a question, but I said, "I don't have a history of drug abuse."

"If you say so."

Clearly she didn't believe me, but why should that bother me? She filled in a few things on the computer and printed me off a receipt.

Don't let the nerves show, I reminded myself, trying to keep myself from fidgeting.

Then she got to her feet to escort me back to Mr. Ramirez's office.

There they were. Two uniformed cops. They were in the hallway, just beyond the water fountain but before the door to Mr. Ramirez's office. One of them was holding a set of handcuffs, jiggling them.

As the receptionist stepped aside to let me precede her, I tried to relax the muscles in my shoulders and take a few deep, regular breaths.

Behind me, her heels clicked on the linoleum floor.

I ducked my head as I went past the cops. Did I think they wouldn't recognize me? My wrists itched in anticipation of the feel of cold steel clamping.

When we passed them, they didn't move.

Now the back of my neck was itching, but I knew better than to look back. I eased into the doorway of Mr. Ramirez's office.

The receptionist turned and her heels clicked in the other direction, then stopped.

"The guy you're looking for is the only one left in the waiting room." She had to be talking to the cops in the hallway.

"Thanks," one of them responded. "Be easier to get him if no one else is there."

I practically fell into the office out of relief.

Mr. Ramirez sat in his ancient wooden desk chair, tipping his huge bulk so far back that I wondered why he didn't tip over, chair and all.

"Sit down, Jesse," he said.

I did so, lowering into the peeling plastic chair on the other side of his desk.

"You got anything you want to tell me?" He tapped his yellowed teeth with the eraser of a pencil.

"Nothing I *want* to tell you."

He raised his bushy graying eyebrows until they practically met his slick black hair.

"But I guess I got things I *ought* to tell you."

He nodded. "Smart decision."

No point in not telling him everything. Any part he didn't know, he could find out easily enough. And he most assuredly would. Always a good idea to have any bad news to a parole officer come directly from the parolee. Otherwise he'll wonder what else I was trying to hide.

"Well, first of all, I got locked up on Friday night."

Montgomery had been in touch with him about that. "Tell me about it."

"This girl I been seeing sometimes, Kelly Mathias, I don't know if I've told you about her?"

"I know a little bit. She works with you. Go on."

"She got raped. And I got picked up for that."

"Did you do it?"

That stung, but what did I expect? "No."

"Were you charged?"

"No. She couldn't talk to the cops at first, but when she could, she told the cops it wasn't me, it was this other guy, Razorback. So they cut me loose."

"And who is Razorback?"

"Somebody she knew through her dad, who just got released from prison. He's using her place as his home plan. So I've been staying away from her place."

"Razorback is his street name, I take it?"

"Yeah."

"You know his real name?"

"No."

"And where is this guy now?"

"I dunno. Nobody seems to have seen him around."

"Know anything else about him?"

I said, "He's a registered sex offender." I wasn't telling him anything he couldn't find out easily enough.

"I take it he's not at his registered address?"

"Probably not. They'd've picked him up if he was."

Mr. Ramirez nodded. "So he's in violation."

"Yep."

"Anything else I should know about?"

I licked my lips. "Kelly's dad—they call him Old Buckles—he says he's trying to figure out what really happened to her."

"Old Buckles is a street name again, yes?"

"Yeah."

"Interesting names."

"Well, they're bikers."

"Belong to a club?"

"Yeah. Predators. You know about them?"

He frowned. "I do indeed. And you shouldn't be hanging around them."

"That's why I been staying away from Kelly's place. 'Cause her place is her dad's home plan for parole."

"What do you think really happened to her?"

I fidgeted in the seat. "Hard to say." I didn't want to go into it, but I figured I'd better. "There's a rumor that Razorback and I had an agreement to swap women."

He paused and put the pencil on his desk. "And did you?"

"No, sir. I wouldn't speak for Kelly. I been trying to stay away from the Predators. And I never had anything to do with Razorback's old lady, Black Rose."

"So who's spreading these rumors?"

"That's what I don't get. Black Rose."

"And what exactly has she been saying?"

"That her and me had sex. Then when Razorback tried to make good on the deal with Kelly, she tried to fight him off."

He nodded. "And you didn't sleep with this Black Rose woman?"

"No, sir."

"Why would she say something like that if it wasn't true?"

"I got no idea."

"Who believes her?"

"Just about everybody she's told, I think."

"Has she told that to Kelly?"

My chest tightened, and I looked down at the floor. "Yeah."

"And does Kelly believe her?"

My eyes were suddenly damp. "Yeah. She don't want no more to do with me."

"Well, if she thinks you told some biker he could have a go at her in exchange for you screwing his lady, why wouldn't she be mad at you?"

"I understand that." I wiped my eye with the back of my hand. "What I don't understand is why she'd believe I'd agree to something like that."

Mr. Ramirez rocked forward in his chair, his short but broad body moving with alarming speed until his chunky hands landed on the desk in front of him. He picked up a pen and chewed on the end. "You really care about this Kelly person, don't you, Jesse?" he asked.

I took a deep breath. "Yes, sir."

"So it's unlikely you'd agree to a deal like that? Especially with someone you *know* is already a sex offender."

Not trusting my voice to hold steady, I nodded. I *hadn't* known that about Razorback, but I wouldn't have agreed anyhow.

"Do you think she'd say you'd been stalking her?"

Lord. That had never occurred to me. "I hope not. I stayed away from her after she told me she didn't want to see me."

"When was that?"

"When I went to see her in the hospital."

His bottomless black eyes narrowed. "And that was after Detective Montgomery told you not to do that?"

Obviously they'd been talking. No point in me denying it. "Yes, sir."

"And since then?"

"Since then, what?"

"You called her? Sent her text messages? E-mailed her?"

"No. I got a phone at home, but I don't got a cell phone, and I don't know how to do e-mail."

"You got a computer?"

Even if I had any notion how to use a computer, I could never afford one. "No."

"You been staying away from convicted felons?"

"As much as I can."

Mr. Ramirez took a manila envelope from a drawer and emptied several photographs on the desk. "Want to tell me about these?"

My stomach cramped, and bile rose in my throat. I hoped I could keep from throwing up. Swallowing hard, I looked at the pictures.

In the first one, there I stood, practically leaning on the handlebars of Old Buckles' trike. In the background were several other Predators. It was a good bet that most, if not all, of them were convicted felons. And a good bet he got the pictures from Carissa.

"That's Old Buckles," I said, pointing at him in the picture.

"I thought you weren't going over to your girlfriend's house because he was over there."

"Well, yeah."

"But you'll meet him in a park known for hooker pickups and drug sales?"

"He came and found me as I was getting off of work."

"You don't get off of work *here*. And it's not on your way home. As a matter of fact, nestled like it is against the fence around the railroad tracks, it's not on the way to *anywhere*."

"Old Buckles met me outside work. I was afraid the company would be mad at me if the bikers were hanging around, so I asked him if we could move. This is where he chose."

"He and the other gang members rode their bikes over there. How did you get there?"

I looked off to the side. A big calendar with red X's through the days that had already passed was on the wall. I wondered if today had been X'd out yet.

Mr. Ramirez leaned forward. "Well?"

"Old Buckles gave me a ride."

"On the back of his bike?"

"Yes, sir."

"Interesting way to stay away from convicted felons."

Miserably, I shrugged.

"But you know, I've looked at these pictures. And I don't see you doing anything you shouldn't. Not taking the smokes, which I'd bet are blunts. Not fighting or looking threatening. And I spoke to the young woman from the newspaper who took them. She said she didn't see you do anything, either. You know who she is?"

I nodded. "Carissa." She didn't care how much trouble she caused for anyone else. If I saw her again, I'd have to just turn and walk away.

"So you know her?"

I swallowed hard again and tried to keep my hands still. "Not really. She says she wants to write a story or something about the Predators."

"What's that got to do with you?"

"She asked if I could take her to the clubhouse."

"What did you tell her?"

"That even if I knew where it was, I didn't think that was a good idea for her to go there."

Mr. Ramirez drummed his stubby fingers on his desk, staring past me. Finally he said, "You've got to realize I'm not happy with the things you're getting involved in."

I took a deep breath that hurt my chest. "Yes, sir."

"Stay away from those bikers. And if a woman doesn't want to see you, stay away from her, too. Even if you think you could explain things to her and change her mind. She's got a right to not be bothered."

"Yes, sir." He was right. I knew he was right. So why was it so hard to convince myself I needed to stay far away from Kelly?

He got to his feet. He stood about five foot two inches tall and about as wide around. "I'll see you next week. Same time. And I hope you'll be able to tell me you've managed to avoid these problems. Or we may have to rethink home detention. Or even parole violation."

"Yes, sir. Thank you."

But I knew I wasn't going to be able to let this whole thing go, even if I wanted to. Which I didn't.

CHAPTER 11

Before Mr. Ramirez could change his mind, I hurried through the waiting room, which was filling up. Not stopping to put my jacket on, I took the stairs two at a time. When I reached the top, I took a deep breath of free air and slipped into my jacket. I cut through the full parking lot next to the police station and out onto the street behind the jail. Now would be a very good time to go home and stay there until I had to go to work.

Court was in session, and the curb was lined with cars, many of them on the super expensive side. Seemed like a lot of rich people had business in the courthouse.

A dark blue Audi cut across the street just in front of me and pulled up onto the ramp leading up to a loading bay at the rear of the building. A tall, lanky figure stepped out from behind the shrubbery and leaned into the driver's window. The driver passed something to him, backed off the ramp, and peeled away.

There was something familiar about the slope of the man's hunched shoulders.

"Willis?"

He looked up at me with panic in his eyes. "Who are you?"

"Come on, it's me. Jesse. I was your cell buddy, just for a night. Last Friday."

"Oh, yeah." He rubbed his nose and looked at the concrete below his feet.

"You make bail?" I asked.

"Nah. They just let me out. Charges dropped."

"Well, that's even better. Your mom must have decided not to make a big deal of the whole thing."

"I guess." He looked at the envelope in his hand. "Where are you headed?"

"Home. I'm coming from the parole office. I got to report once a week."

"How can you work if you got to report in the daytime like that?"

"Night job. Midnight to eight shift."

He looked around. "I need a job."

"Yeah. Jobs come in handy. Especially if you ever expect to need money for anything."

He gave me a weak grin. "When I was gonna be released, they let me call my mom. She wouldn't come pick me up."

"What was she doing?"

"She was at work."

"So she don't want to miss work. It won't hurt you to walk."

"She says she wants me to move out of the house."

"No surprise there. You're not a kid anymore. And you beating up on her boyfriend can't help *that* relationship."

"I haven't got any place to go. Or any money."

"You had the right idea. Get a job."

He looked defeated. "Jobs aren't easy to come by." He was right about that. "And even if I got something right away, it'd be a while before I got paid."

"So go to the Rescue Mission. You can stay there. And look for a job. See if you can't pick up some day labor."

He looked puzzled. "Day labor?"

"Yeah. If you go down to the Mission, they'll know who's hiring casual labor. It's usually hard physical work, and the pay's not great, but you get it at the end of the day. Usually in cash."

"Then what?"

"You do that and keep applying for jobs. When you get enough saved up, you look for a room or a place to share with somebody."

He glanced around. "For now, I've gone back to being a spotter again. I just got ten bucks for calling in a car."

Shaking my head, I said. "Not good. What kinds of cars are they looking for?"

"Well, like that black Lincoln there. It's pretty new. It's in pretty good shape, only a little dent in the hood. And they said they're looking for Lincolns. So I called it in, and they said they had somebody right in the neighborhood, so he stopped and gave me the ten. If they pick it up, it's gonna be another forty."

I looked at the car he was looking at. My stomach got queasy. I was more familiar with that car than I wanted to be. Especially with the hood and how it got its dent. "You know whose car that is?"

"Probably one of the lawyers. They all drive flashy cars. So I told them the driver'll be in the courthouse for a while. A few more hours, at least."

Shaking my head, I said, "I know that car. A couple of police detectives drive it. I bet it was seized in a drug bust. And I bet they put a LoJack on it."

Willis took a step back and covered his mouth.

I asked, "Do you know what the people you're dealing with do with the cars?"

"No. And I don't think I want to."

"They either drive them straight down to the docks at the Baltimore harbor and load them right up to be shipped to Africa or South America, or they take them to a chop shop and break them down for parts."

"But *I* wouldn't be doing any of that."

"Maybe not directly. But it's conspiracy."

"Not really."

"Yes, really. Remember, we talked about conspiracy?"

He pulled his jacket closer and looked away.

"And the guy in the Audi, the one who gave you the tenner?"

He nodded. "I told him about you, too."

I had to struggle to swallow my surprise so it didn't show. "Me?"

"Yeah. He asked if I'd met anybody in jail who might want to make a couple of extra bucks, too. So I told him about you."

Anger shot through me. "Don't you remember I told you how stupid it was to get mixed up in this?"

"I guess. But I need the money."

"For what?"

He shrugged. "Stuff?"

"Drugs?"

"A little. But I ain't no addict."

"You're sure as hell acting like one. Don't give no thought to the dumb things you're doing. Getting somebody else—*me*—mixed up in this. You wanna go down for this stupid shit, nothing I can do about it. But leave me out of it."

He turned away from me. "Too late. I done told him about you."

I clenched my fists. Punching him out wouldn't undo what he'd done. And might get me in real trouble. "What did he say?"

"Not a whole lot. He seemed to know who you were."

I shoved my fist into my jacket pocket and turned to walk away.

"And he did say your girlfriend was going up to the Predators' clubhouse, looking for you."

I whirled around to face him and tried to make sense of that. I couldn't imagine Kelly going up to the clubhouse, especially after what had happened to her. And wasn't she supposed to be in a rehab facility? "Was it a woman by the name of Black Rose, by any chance?"

"No. He specifically said it wasn't Black Rose. It was the other one."

Couldn't be. Not Kelly. My stomach lurched. Was she really looking for me? And why up at the Predators' clubhouse?

"How many girlfriends you got, anyhow?"

"None, really."

I turned, and this time I did walk away. I wasn't going to listen to this nonsense. My throat closed at the idea of Kelly up at the clubhouse. Impossible she'd go there looking for me. He had to be lying.

I wondered if Old Buckles was trying to lure me up there, onto his territory where I'd be at a disadvantage. But that wasn't his style. If he wanted a confrontation, he'd find me. And he wouldn't be secretive about it. He wouldn't worry if it was on the street in front of the police station or at my place or wherever.

I hadn't gotten more than around the corner and a block away before the Audi swooped by again. The brakes squealed as it skidded to a stop a few feet from me.

Right next to the police station and the courthouse. Some people had no sense. Of course, if they had any sense, they wouldn't have Willis "spotting" what he thought were lawyers' cars while court was in session.

The window rolled down. "Hey, Jesse!"

It was Aaron. I *knew* he had no sense. "What?"

"I was just talking to Willis here about you!" He nodded to the passenger seat, where Willis sat.

My fists clenched again, but I forced my hands to stay at my side. "And?"

"He tell you that your girlfriend been looking for you up at the Predators' clubhouse?"

"How do you know?"

"This guy by the name Funky Joe done told me."

"He was probably talking about Black Rose. No way is she my girlfriend."

"That chick that runs the backhoe business? Nah. I mean, she might be up there, the clubhouse is in back of her place, but he said 'the other girlfriend.'"

Funky Joe owed me no favors after I'd left him flattened on the sidewalk at the hospital. Maybe *he* was trying to lure me up to the clubhouse.

Aaron rubbed his nose with his sleeve. "You been screwing one of the biker chicks, too? Wow. You get around."

Why would I even listen to Aaron? He lied all the time, and his brains were so fried on drugs that even if he tried to tell the truth he might not be able to.

But this was *Kelly* we were talking about. "How come she was looking for me up there? I don't go there, and she knows that."

Aaron shrugged. "You wanna go ask Funky Joe?"

"Not especially. And I got no idea where he is."

He grinned. "I do. He works at that bridge construction site out by the highway. A couple of the Predators do. I had to go by there anyhow."

"Why do you got to 'go by there anyhow'?"

He pursed his lips and tapped his cheek with one tobacco-stained forefinger. I think that was supposed to make him look wise, but he just succeeded in looking crazier than usual. "I got business to take care of with him. You could ride with me."

I sized up the car. "And get caught riding in a stolen car?"

Aaron managed to look mildly insulted. "It ain't *stolen*. I *borrowed* it."

"From somebody who stole it?"

"No! I told you. I got some new business partners. They said they didn't want me riding around in that old pickup of mine while I'm on business. So they let me use one of their cars."

"Is their business boosting cars, by any chance?"

"They got lots of stuff going. I'm not sure exactly what they do. I take phone calls and pass on messages and deliver money. Like I just done now." He nodded toward Willis. They made a good pair. One was dumber than the other, but it wasn't obvious which was which.

"And they're hooked up with the Predators?"

"Well, some of them might be. I don't think the big boss is a biker, though. He just uses them sometimes. Protection, like, 'cause nobody much messes with them."

None of this sounded good.

Aaron scratched a scab on his scrawny neck. "You wanna go talk to Funky Joe or not? I got to get there while they're on lunch."

"Don't Old Buckles work the same job?"

"Yeah."

So far I'd done all right with Old Buckles. I didn't really want to push my luck with him. I figured my best plan was to stay away from him. My gut twisted.

Best plan felt lame. This was *Kelly* we were talking about. If she was really looking for me, I had to find out.

"Okay. But don't think I'm gonna go up to the clubhouse with you. I just wanna ask Funky Joe about it." Assuming that after our last encounter, Funky Joe would talk to me.

And if he was at the construction job, he couldn't be trying to lure me up to the clubhouse.

Aaron grinned. "Climb in. Willis, you got to ride in back."

Willis slid into the back while I walked around and got in the front passenger seat.

We laid rubber once again as we sped off. I looked uneasily back at the police parking lot, but I didn't see anybody preparing to follow us.

Driving a car like this had to be fun. Aaron was enjoying it. He stared straight ahead through the windshield, his gaunt face intense.

We wound through a new section of McMansions that had been built out by the edge of town before the economy crashed. A whole bunch of them sported "For Sale" signs, and some looked abandoned.

A crew was at work in the front yard of one of them, laying pipe in a trench dug from the house to the street.

As we approached the construction site, Aaron took the last turn too fast. I closed my eyes, expecting the car to flip. But it hugged the ground and sent up a spray of gravel as Aaron skidded to a stop next to a cluster of pickups and two choppers parked next to the construction fence. He was living dangerously—if the gravel dented any of them, especially the bikes, somebody wasn't going to be happy with him.

The only activity on the site was a backhoe operator, cutting into a mound of dirt piled partway down a slope to the river.

A man and a woman, both in pristine fluorescent yellow safety vests and hard hats, were carrying on an animated conversation just outside the construction trailer. The woman unrolled a large piece of paper, and they both examined it. She pointed at it, and the man jabbed a pencil where she pointed.

A handful of workers sat on concrete forms, hard hats next to them and lunch boxes open in front of them. Funky Joe was among them, and he looked up as we pulled in. He and another man stood and walked over to the car. They were also wearing yellow safety vests over insulated coveralls, but theirs were battered and dirty.

Aaron rolled down the window. "Hey, guys!"

Funky Joe leaned into the window. "Whadya want?"

"Just stopping by to see if you guys got anything more for me to do."

The biker shook his head. "Not that I know of. But it ain't me in charge."

"Where is everybody else?" Aaron asked.

Funky Joe shook his head. "Damn TCI stopped work on this section, so a lot of the guys left. We ain't working, we don't get paid."

"What's a TCI?"

"Transportation Construction Inspector. She said the drainage slopes were off and that the silt snakes and fences were in the wrong place. Don't see how that can be—there was another TCI here yesterday when we quit for the day, and he said everything was okay. You'd think if the guy last night passed it, it'd be okay for this woman this morning. Bitch."

"So you guys aren't working?"

"There was some stuff we could do on the other side. So a couple of us stayed. But it's pretty much done now, and we got the silt snakes where she says they got to be. Until that backhoe operator gets that slope the way the TCI wants it, we can't work. That'll take most of the afternoon. I'm gonna take off, too."

So far he hadn't paid any attention to me or Willis. "Hey, Funky Joe," I said.

He glared at me, rubbing a bruise on his cheek. "What the hell you want?"

"Aaron here says somebody was looking for me?"

"Yeah. That girlfriend of yours. She was looking for somebody to give her a ride up to the clubhouse. Thought you might be up there."

"Why the hell did she think that?"

A mean smirk covered his face. "I dunno. But I *know* Black Rose was up there. And she says if Razorback don't put in an appearance pretty soon, she's gonna see if she can't hook up with you. So it might get interesting up there when them two bitches get together."

My gut lurched. *Two women getting into it over me? One of them somebody I didn't even know. What was going on here? Didn't seem like that could happen.*

Joe grinned. "I'd like to see *that* fight."

I'd seen plenty of fights in my life, most of them over something stupid. But I couldn't even begin to imagine Kelly and Black Rose getting into it. Kelly, at least, was much too sensible. And wasn't she supposed to be going to rehab for an injured shoulder? She'd be in no shape to take on anyone, even if she did outweigh Black Rose by maybe fifty pounds.

Unless somebody brought a gun or a knife to the fight. Kelly wouldn't do that.

How well did I really know Kelly, though? I thought uneasily. Not nearly as well as I thought I did. They say love is blind.

Love. Where did that come from? The word hit me upside the head.

Did I *love* Kelly? Was that what all this pain and anguish was about? I liked her, sure, and the sex was great. But here I was, hanging out with people who I knew could get me in trouble and thinking about doing stupid things when I knew a lot better. But I *had* to find out whether Kelly wanted to see me or not. Was that what love did to a person? Funky Joe was looking at me like I was some kind of insect he was thinking maybe he should step on.

I bit my lip. "You know what she wanted to see me about?"

He grinned again. "Nope. That'd be between the two of you. But y'know, a woman scorned and all that."

I took a deep breath. "How long ago was that?"

"Not long. If she went up there, I bet she's there now."

Common sense said this might be a set up. For me, at least. "She know where it is? It can't be easy to find."

Funky Joe gave me a mean grin. "She had a pretty good idea. But I made sure she knew how to get up there."

Thinking for a minute, I asked, "Old Buckles up there now?"

Funky Joe shrugged. "He took off as soon as he knew we wouldn't be working a whole shift. But I don't know where he went. I got nothing to do with none of this. Not with the cars and not with the broads." He straightened up, spit on the ground, and went back to his lunch.

"Well." Aaron rolled up the window. "I guess I got to get this car up there and see if they got anything else for me to do. You guys coming along?"

"I got nothing better to do," Willis said.

The ache in my gut turned to a cold lump. Against my better judgment, I said, "Yeah." *What was I getting myself involved in?*

The twisting blacktop road narrowed and turned to gravel as it climbed into the hills.

A pickup pulling a trailer with a small backhoe on it passed us. The windows in the pickup were tinted, and I couldn't see if it was Black Rose at the wheel. If it was, at least I wouldn't have to worry about her and Kelly fighting while I was up there.

We crossed a bridge that had seen better days and made an abrupt left on to a wide gravel driveway. Inside the car, we bounced around. I was surprised such an expensive car didn't have a smoother suspension, even on the rough surface. But I guess it was built for the German Autobahn, not Appalachian back roads.

After a short drive through the woods, we came out in a cleared area dominated by a huge cinderblock building, one side lined with garage doors. A rusting trailer with a sign that said, "General Trenching and Excavating" was off to one side. Sagging overhead wires led to both the building and the trailer.

Only two choppers were parked on the gravel apron in front along with a battered pickup truck I thought I recognized as Aaron's. I hoped that meant there weren't a lot of bikers hanging around. I could do without the group dynamics here, especially if Old Buckles wasn't around to keep a handle on things.

Aaron drove straight toward the building and slammed on the brakes at the last minute, squealing to a stop just inches from one of the closed garage doors. One of these days his show-off driving was going to get him in real trouble. But I hoped it would be at a time when I wasn't in the vehicle he was driving.

A man stepped out of the building, buttoning his shirt as he came toward us. His arms were massive and tattooed, a cigarette dangling from his fingertips. He stopped and crossed his arms over his chest, watching as Aaron got out of the car. I watched the cigarette with fascination. How did he manage to hang onto it without either dropping it or burning himself?

"Hey, Butch. Where's Smokey?" Aaron asked.

Butch swayed slightly as he stood, reaching out one massive arm to steady himself on the doorframe. His unkempt beard covered half of his hefty chest, and he had a slightly disoriented look on his face. "He ain't here. Who'd you bring with you?"

Maybe that wasn't a straight tobacco cigarette in his hand? More likely a joint. Or even a wet, a combination of tobacco, weed, and angel dust. That could lead to pretty unpredictable behavior.

Aaron gestured back toward the car. "The one in the back seat's Willis. He's one of our spotters."

"Yeah? And why'd you bring him up here?"

Aaron shrugged. "I dunno. See if there's any more work, I guess."

Butch gestured toward me and almost fell over. He must have been really wasted. "And the other guy?"

"He's looking for his girlfriend. Somebody told her he was up here. So he come to get her. Or something."

"Really?"

I got out of the car. "Is she up here?"

"If she is, she came 'cause she wanted to see us. Not you. So you can just get going."

I squared my shoulders and looked straight into his watery bottomless eyes. "I'd like to talk to her."

He rocked back on the heels of his boots and put the cigarette or joint or whatever back in his mouth, not saying anything. He inhaled deeply.

A whiff of ammonia mixed with the combined scent of tobacco and marijuana from his smoke. More likely a hand-rolled blunt than a cigarette. *Were they running a meth lab up here? Wouldn't surprise me.*

A female scream came from inside the building and resonated through the clearing. It didn't sound like Kelly's voice, but I'd never heard Kelly scream.

"I'd like to talk to her," I repeated.

The guy shrugged. He pinched out the end of his smoke and said to Aaron, "You best be putting that car inside." Then he turned to me and looked me over.

I didn't flinch.

He shrugged. "What name you want me to give?"

"Jesse."

Raising his eyebrows, he said, "That's it?"

"Yep."

"Wait here." When Aaron got the garage door open, Butch stepped through and disappeared into the dimness inside.

I stayed where I was, but peered into the gloom.

A number of newish cars stood around in various stages of disassembly. A chop shop. Aaron had been stupid to bring other people up here. And I'd been stupid to come.

No wonder Old Buckles didn't want to spend time up here. Even if he wasn't worried about violating parole himself, he wouldn't want his PO to come sniffing around.

I needed to get out of here. Fast. If that *was* Kelly who screamed, I was going to get her out of here. Assuming she wanted to come.

Another garage door opened, and Butch came out, dragging a woman by the arm.

Not Kelly. Carissa. *Talk about being stupid. Once I'd found out it wasn't Black Rose who was looking for me, I hadn't bothered to make sure they were talking about Kelly.*

CHAPTER 12

"This who you was talking about?" the man asked.

I looked at Carissa. She was sobbing, mascara streaking down her face. Her mini dress was ripped, exposing a miniscule frilly bra, which was pulled askew and wouldn't have covered her breasts if they'd been any bigger than mosquito bites.

She'd managed to hang onto something she clutched in her hand. A cell phone? I was willing to bet she couldn't get a signal up here.

"Not really. I was thinking Kelly Mathias."

He snorted. "Old Buckles' girl? She don't come up here. He prob'ly wouldn't let her if she wanted to."

That made more sense to me. I felt like a weight had been lifted from my chest.

But here I was, in a very awkward place and situation for no good reason I could think of.

"You want to take this one anyhow?" he asked. "She said she wanted to party, but she's not much fun. Them long fingernails can do a number on your face. And we got a lot of work to do."

Carissa launched herself at me, still sobbing wildly. "Jesse! You've got to get me out of here."

She slammed into my chest and started to slip to the ground. She was wearing only one of her spiked heels.

I put an arm around her to hold her up. "I guess," I said. Even though I wasn't entirely sure how I was getting out of here myself, I didn't see how I could leave her. Eventually they'd get done with whatever they were doing—looked like removing salable parts from stolen luxury cars—and more Predators would show up. Then they'd be likely to put some effort into holding Carissa down for the "party" she'd asked for.

Although now that she had some idea of what she'd asked for, it was pretty obvious she didn't want it.

She buried her face in my shirt. I only had a few decent shirts, and I wondered if the makeup would wash out.

Aaron came out of the garage, Willis trailing behind him.

"You got wheels?" I asked him.

"My truck." He nodded toward the battered blue pickup.

"Let's get going." Before the bikers thought better of letting us leave.

"Only room for three people in the cab," Aaron said, looking at the four of us.

I shoved Carissa up into an uneven standing position. "Willis, you ride in the truck bed."

A very appropriately frightened look crossed his face, but Willis stepped up on the rear bumper and heaved himself in.

Carissa tried to brush the tangle of hair out of her face. "I need my other shoe and my coat."

"You probably got more shoes. And another coat. We don't have enough time to get them, so just forget about them."

She'd been battered and probably sexually assaulted. Why couldn't she understand how precarious our situation was? We needed to get out of there.

Aaron stood uncertainly, his keys in his hand. A drop of blood trickled from one swollen and reddened nostril. "But I haven't got the money for delivering the car. Can't I wait until Smokey and the other guys get here?"

"You can pick it up later. Get in the truck." I hoped he could drive. We'd have to chance it.

He walked around to the driver's side and climbed in.

I opened the passenger door. Carissa just stood there. I picked her up and shoved her onto the seat, then got in beside her and shut the door. And locked it.

Aaron fumbled with the keys.

Two other men stepped out of the garage, one of them zipping up his pants. The other one held a shop rag held up to his face. It was turning red with blood. "Where's that damn bitch?" he asked.

I said to Aaron, "Start the damn truck and let's get out of here."

"Huh?" He looked up at me.

"You want me to drive?" I didn't have a driver's license, and I could get in a lot of trouble if I was caught behind the wheel, but I had a feeling it would be nothing next to what might happen if these three guys thought through what was going on. Or if more of the Predators showed up while we were still here.

"Nah." He finally got the key in the ignition and shifted into gear. We lurched forward, the truck threatening to stall.

The engine finally caught, and we careened down the driveway. I held onto Carissa to keep her from bouncing into Aaron as he drove. I hoped Willis had found some way to hang on, but I wasn't going to ask Aaron to stop the truck so I could check.

We continued on the gravel road and finally turned onto the black-top, where the ride settled down a bit. As we went around a curve, we met a group of bikers coming in our direction who took up most of the road. Aaron veered onto the shoulder, and they swept by us.

Carissa was still crying and shaking. I turned up the heat in the truck, but she still must have been freezing. I suppose the gallant thing to do would have been to offer her my jacket, but I couldn't see what good that would do. Besides, she'd gotten herself into that fix.

"Where's your car?" I asked her. A coat and a shoe I could see aban-doning, but if her car was somewhere up at the clubhouse, she'd have to retrieve it some way.

She sniffed. "I left it at the park."

"Which park? One in town?"

She didn't answer.

I tried again. "The one where we were the other day?"

She nodded, sobs choking her voice. "Yes. I figured it was a good place to look for some of the Predators."

That was probably true. The park was well known as an open air drug market, and while the Predators probably would not involve them-selves in street-level sales to people they didn't know, it would come as no surprise to find out they were major suppliers of meth to the dealers who hung around there. Aaron knew which park we were talking about. Without saying anything, he turned in that direction.

"How'd you get up to the clubhouse?" I asked.

Carissa sniffed. "When I saw one of the bikers, I went over and asked him if I could go up and see it. At first he didn't want to take me, but I told him I was looking for you."

"Why'd that convince him to take you up there?"

"I told him that you'd said there'd be a big party up there and I could go if I wanted."

"Then what'd he say?"

"He asked if I wanted to party."

"And?"

"And I said sure, that's what I wanted to go up for. So he made a few calls on his cell phone and said there'd be a party up there later today."

Closing my eyes and sighing, I said, "I *told* you I didn't hang out up there. And I told you a party at a biker clubhouse wouldn't be something you'd like."

She tried to pull a simpering look, but it was a lot less effective with her mascara streaking down her cheeks. And when she gave her head that little toss, her matted and tangled hair didn't do its little flip. "I thought you were just saying that to scare me."

Why would I want to scare her? I said, "Then what happened?"

"He asked if I *really* wanted to party. I said sure. He asked how much—I didn't really want to *pay* him to get a story, so I just asked if he could tell me how to get there. He said he'd give me a ride, right now, and I could just stay up there until everybody else got there, so I got on his bike."

I shook my head. "He figured you were out whoring and was trying to find out how much you would charge for a gang bang."

She sat up straighter. "What?"

"They'd be willing to pay something, either in cash or more likely drugs, but it's not a deal you'd be likely to want to take."

"I never said I'd *sleep* with any of them."

"What do you think their definition of a party would be? They thought that's what you were offering."

"Well." She tossed her head. "I won't say I'd never put out for a story—it can give you a really unique perspective—but they were *hurting* me. They were awfully rough."

"They tend to be."

We arrived at the park, and Aaron pulled up next to the puke-green car. Carissa and I got out.

Willis climbed out of the bed, his face pale and his hands shaking. "Thanks, Jesse," he said. "I think maybe I'll go see if my mom will let me stay for a few days while I look for a regular job."

I nodded. "Good idea. Otherwise try the Rescue Mission."

"Maybe I'll do that." He turned and made his way down the street.

Aaron leaned out the window. "You guys gonna be okay?"

"Yeah. And thanks for the ride."

"You don't think the Predators are gonna be mad at me 'cause I brought you and Willis up to the clubhouse, do you?"

I thought for a few seconds. "My guess is that those guys aren't going to say anything about it. They seemed pretty wasted. And they let Carissa go. When they think about it, they won't want to admit they handled it so badly. Including letting me and Willis see the operation."

"Hope you're right. I never thought of it like that," he said. If Aaron had ever been capable of coherent thought, the drugs had pretty much addled that ability right out of his mind.

"So don't *you* say nothing about it," I said to him, although I knew he couldn't be trusted.

"Okay." He rolled up the window and slammed the truck into gear.

Carissa stood there, tilting to the side where she didn't have a shoe. She patted the sides of her dress, a stricken look on her face. "My car keys are in my coat pocket."

I sighed. "I hope you didn't leave your purse up there."

"No. I took my keys and a twenty dollar bill and stuck them in my pocket. I didn't think I wanted to have my credit cards and checkbook with me. Just my smartphone in case I wanted to call somebody. But it wouldn't work."

Not bringing her purse with her was maybe the first intelligent thought she'd had.

"What am I going to do?"

I sure wasn't going to try to break into her car. "You got somebody you could call?"

"Yes." She was still holding the phone and tried to punch in a number.

"This doesn't work." She looked at it in dismay.

"Maybe it got knocked around too much."

"Maybe. Can I borrow yours?"

"Don't have one," I said.

She looked like she didn't believe me. "*Everybody's* got a cell phone."

"Guess I'm not 'everybody.'"

A car pulled around the corner and stopped next to us. A black Lincoln. I closed my eyes and took a deep breath. This was not likely to go well.

Montgomery and Belkins both got out.

I looked around. No way to get out of here.

Belkins tore the unlit cigar out of his mouth. "Just what the hell is going on here?"

Carissa gave him a calculating look, then tried to flip her tangled mop of blond hair off her face and launched herself at Belkins, tears flowing freely again.

"I'm so glad you're here!" she simpered. "I'm so scared. And cold."

Belkins actually got a tender look on his face. He put his arms around her and said, "There's a blanket in the back of the car. Shall I get it for you?"

"Yes," she sobbed.

Montgomery and I both stared as he opened the back door and pulled the blanket out, wrapping it around her. "It's cold out here. Don't you have a coat?" he asked.

Pulling the blanket close around her, Carissa collapsed onto his chest. "I *asked* him to get it for me." She gestured toward me. "But he wouldn't. Or get my shoe. And now I don't have a car key. It was in my coat pocket."

Belkins glared at me. "Too much trouble to get the lady's things for her, was it, Damon?"

To Carissa, he said, "Did he do this to you, beat up you up like this?"

I didn't think she was really beaten up too badly, but her makeup was a mess.

"No. But he wouldn't help, either."

Montgomery jumped in. "What did happen?"

She sniffed a few times. "You know I'm a reporter for the *Rothsburg Register*? I was working on a story. Up at the Predators' clubhouse."

"You were up at the Predators' clubhouse?"

"Yes."

"Did Damon take you up there?"

"No. He's the one who brought me back here. Him and a few of his friends. But my *stuff's* still up there."

Montgomery belatedly stirred himself. "Jesse. Hands on your head. Fingers interlaced."

I followed his directions, and he did a half-hearted pat-down, but didn't remove my wallet and keychain.

"What were you doing up at the Predators' clubhouse?" he asked me.

I shook my head. "Somebody told me my girlfriend was up there looking for me. I thought they meant Kelly."

"That's not a smart place to be when you're on parole."

"Tell me about it. It's not a smart place to be even if I'm *not* on parole."

"You know, it's no secret that we've been keeping an eye on that place."

No surprise there.

"You can take your hands down," Montgomery said. "How'd you get up to the clubhouse?"

I thought for a minute. I didn't want to throw Aaron under the bus after he'd been the one who gave us a way out of there. But I was pretty sure Aaron was one of the ways they were keeping an eye on it. Unless I was sorely mistaken, he was a police informant. Of course he'd tell them all about it. I'd better be careful, or I'd tell them all kinds of conflicting things. They'd catch me on all of them.

So I said, "Aaron gave me a ride."

"In his truck?"

"His truck was up there, and we came back in it. But he was driving a blue Audi. He put that in the garage." I was pretty sure I wasn't telling him anything he didn't already know or wouldn't find out anyhow.

"Anything you want to tell me about what was going on up there?"

"Not really. Just some miscommunication. I thought I'd find Kelly, not Carissa, up there. And Carissa was up there 'cause she wanted to do a story on the Predators. I don't think she had any idea what she was getting herself into when she said she'd like to party with them."

Belkins turned toward her. "Of course not. How could she? She's just a young kid."

Montgomery followed his gaze. "Looks like she was getting more than she bargained for."

I nodded. "I'd say that's a safe bet."

We watched as Belkins tucked Carissa in the back seat of the Lincoln and wrapped the blanket around her. The cell phone was still held securely in her hand.

Montgomery adjusted the angle of his hat. "Looks to me like we're going to take her home to get another car key."

I nodded. "Didn't know Belkins had a helpful side."

Montgomery smiled and said, "I don't think you're likely to ever see it yourself. But he's got a soft spot for little blonde girls in trouble. You know he had a daughter who was murdered?"

"I'd heard something about that."

"And she was killed by a serial sex offender who was released on parole before his sentence was up."

"Is that why he's so sure I shouldn't have been paroled?"

"Big part of it."

"I'm not a sex offender. And the victim in my case was a male drug dealer, not a girl."

"Don't think it makes much difference to him. A killer's a killer."

I saw no point in saying I hadn't actually killed anybody myself. My conviction spoke for itself.

And made me a prime suspect whenever there was an investigation of a crime that touched anyone around me.

CHAPTER 13

After the shift broke on Friday morning, I had to wait for Jim, the foreman, to bring my paycheck. Almost everybody else had direct deposit. Someday maybe I'd open a bank account, when I could be sure I could maintain a minimum balance so they wouldn't take a service charge every month. Until then, I dealt in cash with the occasional money order.

When I stepped out the gate into the watery winter sunlight, the other workers on my shift had all left, but a distressingly familiar black Lincoln was parked next to the fire hydrant.

I closed my eyes and sighed. Pulling my hands out of my pockets, I stopped and waited.

This was the third time in a week somebody'd been waiting for me to get out of work. Maybe I needed to start leaving through the truck yard or something.

But they'd just find me another time.

The car doors opened. Montgomery and Belkins stepped out and approached me.

Belkins spit on the sidewalk. "You know the routine, Damon. Assume the position."

I glanced at Montgomery. "The wall or the hood of the car?"

Montgomery laughed. "The wall, I think. The car's still got a dent in the hood from the last time."

Turning and putting the palms of my hands on the dirty bricks of the factory wall, I spread my feet and leaned onto my hands, looking under my arm to try to keep an eye on them. Especially Belkins.

He sauntered over and lifted a foot toward mine, as if he were going to kick my foot further back. He stopped, glanced at my steel-toed work boots, and took a step back.

Montgomery came up behind me. He ran his hands under my jacket, between my legs and over my pockets. He unclipped my wallet from my belt and removed my key from my jeans pocket. Then he cuffed my hands behind me.

"Turn around and face me."

I did so, but I didn't look him in the eyes. *What now?*

Belkins stepped up and moved his face right up to mine. His breath had the sour odor of last night's whiskey. Or maybe it was this morning's. "What do you know about one Harvey McGillian?" he asked.

The name meant nothing at all to me. "Not a thing," I said.

"I find that hard to believe." He sprayed spittle on my cheek.

Since I didn't know what he was talking about, I didn't say anything.

"Come on," Belkins said, backing up a bit and taking one of his squat cigars from his pocket. "Don't play dumb with me."

"Don't know who that is," I said.

He unwrapped the cigar. "You can't tell me you don't know the members of the Predators who hang around your girlfriend's house."

No point is saying that if Kelly ever had been my girlfriend, she certainly wasn't now. "I try to keep my distance from them," I said. "Most of them are convicted felons. It would violate my parole."

Belkins snorted. "And I suppose going up to their clubhouse doesn't constitute a violation?"

"You're right. I could be violated for that."

"So why'd you do it?"

Of course they knew about that. I'd been with Aaron. "I thought Kelly was up there looking for me."

Montgomery took over. "I thought I told you to stay away from that woman. And I bet your PO told you the same thing. Didn't he?"

I gave a slight nod.

"I want to hear you say it."

"Both you and Mr. Ramirez told me to stay away from Kelly," I dutifully replied.

"And?"

"*If* she didn't want to see me."

"What made you think she wanted to see you?"

He had me there. "Somebody told me that."

"Told you what?"

"That my girlfriend was up at the clubhouse because she thought I was going up there."

"And what would make her think you'd be up at the clubhouse?"

"I dunno."

"Because you were up there a lot?"

"No. That was the first time." I'd better be careful of what I said. I still didn't know what they were getting at, but I knew I'd better not let them catch me in a lie. Or blurt out something they could twist to use against me.

"Were you looking for drugs? I understand they can get up a pretty good shake-and-bake temporary meth lab up there."

I remembered the ammonia scent. "Wouldn't surprise me. But I don't use."

He raised his eyebrows. "I've heard to the contrary."

Was that Aaron's doing? I was tempted to say, "So go test my piss," but he'd be likely to go through Mr. Ramirez, and I'd end up having to pay for it.

Montgomery was continuing to stare at me. "And I don't deal," I added, in case that was what Aaron had told them.

Montgomery changed tactics. "Is Kelly out of the hospital?"

"I dunno."

"Yet you say you went up to the clubhouse looking for her."

"Yeah. That was pretty stupid. I should have checked to see if she was still in the hospital before I went up there. Or in rehab."

Belkins chewed on the end of his unlit cigar. "You don't know where she is? You don't even make a very good stalker."

I winced.

"And what about that poor girl who was up there?" He took the soggy cigar out of his mouth.

It was hard for me to think of Carissa as a "poor girl." I flexed my shoulders, trying to keep the blood circulation going through my hands. "I didn't know it was her who was up there."

He put his blotchy red face inches from me. His rank breath filled my nose. "I suppose it was her you went up there to see? Did you think *she* was your girlfriend? Just because she asked you to help her when she was trying to write a story on the Predators? She's got too much class to look twice at *you*."

She sure didn't act like she had any class at all. But I wasn't about to suggest that to Belkins. He waved the cigar in my face. It didn't smell much better than his breath. "What kind of an egotist are you anyhow, thinking you're God's gift to women? Kelly, that woman they call Black Rose, and now Carissa? I bet you're HIV positive, and you're spreading disease. Maybe hepatitis C, too. That's rampant in prison."

It wasn't a stretch to realize that prison inmates were high risk. But I'd never engaged in risky behavior, neither before I was locked up nor in prison, and I'd been tested for HIV upon my release. I'd never used intravenous drugs, and I wasn't about to start now. Kelly was the only woman I'd ever slept with, so unless she was infected and hadn't told me, I could be pretty sure I was still disease-free.

Montgomery looked on in amusement as Belkins continued to rant at me. "What did you do to that girl?"

"Nothing."

"Nothing? Did you see what she looked like?"

"She looked like that when I got up there. I took her away from there. *She* told you that."

"With only one shoe and no coat."

"Didn't seem like a good idea to stay to look for them. We got out while the getting was good. Before any more of the bikers showed up."

"And did you drive?"

"No. I don't have a license. That guy Aaron. You know him."

"And you expect me to believe that you didn't lay a hand on her?"

"Did she *say* I laid a hand on her?"

"No. She says you got her out of there. And she has a misplaced sense of guilt about the whole situation. So she's probably not telling me the whole truth. I think she's trying to shield you. Gratitude you don't deserve." He spit on the ground next to my boot.

I didn't think Carissa's feelings of guilt were particularly misplaced. She had gotten herself into that mess and dragged me into it, after I'd tried to warn her off. And now I was in some kind of trouble because of it.

Belkins drew his bulk up to his full five foot nine inches and tried to glower at me. I tried to look as non-threatening and non-confrontational as I could.

He raised his hand toward me face. I braced myself and closed my eyes.

But the blow didn't come.

I opened my eyes and looked. Montgomery had Belkins by the arm and was leading him back toward the car. "Stop it," he said. "Now. We're not going to jeopardize this case because you lost control."

I kept a wary eye on them and tried to back up a few steps, ending up against the wall.

Belkins stayed next to the car, fuming. Montgomery told him, "Stand still," and came back to face me.

He stood inches from me and leaned down toward me. "You were told to stay away from the Predators."

I nodded.

"But you didn't. Am I right?"

"Yes, sir."

"At least you're being honest with me on this. Carissa, the newspaper lady, she's got pictures of you with the bikers."

"Not over at Kelly's house, though," I pointed out. As if that'd make any difference.

"No. At the park. What were you doing?"

"Talking."

"About what?"

I sighed. No matter how I said this, it was going to be incriminating. "You know who Old Buckles is?"

"Kelly's dad?"

"Yeah. He wanted to talk to me about to the attack on Kelly."

"Why?"

"He was trying to figure out exactly what happened to her." So was I.

"Was he threatening to take revenge?"

That was exactly what he was doing, but I wasn't going to say that. "He just wanted to know. He was pretty upset. Wouldn't you be, if it was your daughter got raped?"

He ignored that. I didn't know if he had a daughter or not. "And he thought you had something to do with it? Directly or indirectly?"

"He didn't know for sure. He was just asking around."

"Seems like he must have a pretty good idea. You sleep with one of the biker chicks? Black Rose?"

"No."

"Then why would she say you did?"

I shook my head but had no answer to give him. I hadn't figured that one out at all.

Montgomery put a slim dark finger under my chin and lifted my head so he could look me in the eyes. "Tell me about what was going on up at the clubhouse when you went up there."

"Not too much. Only a couple of guys there. Looked like they were working on cars."

"Carissa was up there, too?"

"Yeah. She was there."

"Why do you think she wanted to leave with you?"

"I don't think she really had any idea what she was getting herself into when she went up there. One of the bikers asked her if she wanted to party, and she said yes. So he gave her a ride up to the clubhouse." I left out the part about anybody paying anything, either way.

"What do you think they meant by partying?"

"I *know* they meant sex."

"With her?"

"Yes."

"*All* of them?"

"Anyone who was up there."

Montgomery's dark eyes continued to bore into mine. "So why do you think they let her leave with you?"

"Well, there were only three of them. She'd scratched the holy hell out of one of them. They said she wasn't being much fun." And they were so high they couldn't think straight, but I wasn't going to bring that up.

Montgomery backed up a step. "She did get some really good pictures."

I hadn't seen her camera. "I wouldn't know about that."

"On her cell phone. Probably enough for us to get a search warrant. Both for stolen vehicles and running a shake-and-bake operation."

He removed his hand from my chin but continued to peer at me. "You been buying drugs from them?"

Back to that again. "No."

"Supplying them?"

Damn Aaron and his stories. "No."

I knew they were asking similar questions, circling back to the same issues, trying to get me to contradict myself.

Belkins lurched up, looking incredulous. "Let me get this straight. You aren't involved with the Predators and their drug trade."

"No."

Montgomery stepped between us. "Let's get back to the basic reason we stopped you. Do you deny knowing Harvey McGillian?"

"No idea who you're talking about."

Montgomery raised a well-shaped eyebrow. "How about a biker called Razorback?"

My gut tightened. "He's the one who…" I let my voice trail off.

"Who what?"

I took a deep breath. "Raped Kelly."

Belkins made that snorting noise again. "Very good, Damon. Now you got it."

"I don't know him," I said. "Don't think I've ever seen him."

Montgomery looked at me intently. "But you know *of* him."

"I guess."

"What do you know about him?"

"He rides with the Predators. He has a little excavation business—trenches for sewer line connections and stuff. Site preparation for new construction, maybe."

"Know anything else about him?"

"Black Rose is his old lady."

Montgomery glanced at Belkins. "And you do know Black Rose a little better than you seem to know Razorback?" he asked me.

"Not really," I said.

Belkins shifted the cigar to the other hand. "When was the last time you saw him?"

"I don't think I ever saw him."

"Come on, now. Don't outright *lie* to us."

"Honest." Probably that was the wrong word to use. "I've never met him. If I ever saw him, I didn't know it was him."

"You really expect me to believe that?" Belkins looked disgusted.

Montgomery rubbed one of his gloved hands against the other. "We've been looking pretty hard for him. You know nobody seems to have seen Razorback since the night after he roughed Kelly up?"

"No. Old Buckles may have been looking for him. But I was locked up that night. Remember?"

Belkins glared. "You had a few hours." He changed tactics. "You must be pretty pissed about what he did to your girlfriend."

"Well, yeah." I couldn't deny that. No point going into the part about her not really being my girlfriend.

"So you decided to take care of it yourself, did you?"

"No."

"What would you say if I told you we'd found him?" Montgomery asked me.

"I'd say you should lock him up, and he'd be likely safer in the county jail than he would be out on the streets. Or in prison."

"Why would you say that?"

"'Cause some people are pretty pissed at him." I thought about Old Buckles, who had plenty of his buddies both on the street and in the prison system.

"Like you?"

"I'm not gonna do anything to him." At least nothing that might be traced to me and get me locked up again.

"Suppose I told you he wasn't in such good shape when we found him?"

"I'd say he deserved whatever happened to him."

Montgomery grimaced. "I almost hate to tell you this, Jesse, but…"

Belkins cut in. "Jesse Damon, I'm placing you under arrest for the murder of Harvey McGillian, also known as Razorback."

* * * *

Carrying the bedding that I'd been issued, I was escorted to my assigned cell. K-pod again. High security. No surprise there. Once again, the cell had only one other occupant. They must be low on high-security inmates. My cellmate was lying on his bunk, his face to the wall. Maybe asleep. He didn't move when the door slid open, and I stepped in. I put my stuff on the top bunk on the other side, trying to be quiet so I didn't wake him up.

The door slammed shut. I've never heard any other sound like that, the definitive clang of a cell door closing behind me, the lock snicking tight.

The CO sat at the desk in the unused dayroom, his feet propped up and his radio at hand. He looked sleepy, but I wasn't fooled. He was monitoring everything that went on in the cellblock.

The cell was at the end of the row. Since I'd been processed before the jail went into nighttime lockdown mode, they'd had access to the whole range of sizes in stored jumpsuits, and I'd been issued a one that more or less fit. At least I didn't have to keep grabbing the neck of it to keep it from slipping off my shoulder.

After I'd made my bed and stashed the contents of my hygiene kit, I sat on a bottom bunk, rereading my charging papers. Like I wasn't sure what they said. The distinctive scent of the carbonless copy paper tickled my nose.

Confused thoughts churned in my head, none of them helpful. How was Kelly? What kind of evidence did they have that made them think I'd killed Razorback? How likely was it that the state's attorney would seek the death penalty? Why did Black Rose insist that I'd had sex with her? What lies had Aaron told them?

My stomach churned, too.

There was that jail cell trauma welling up inside me again. Reading the charges over and over again didn't help. Especially worrying was the bit about first degree murder and reserving the right to file a capital case. I'd been through similar situations before, but it didn't get any easier with repetition. Bile rose in my throat. I hoped I could keep from throwing up.

My cellmate stirred. He stretched and rolled over, rubbing his eyes with the backs of his hands like a little kid waking up from a nap.

His face was bruised and swollen. Was that a requirement for being assigned to K-pod?

He sat up and looked at me. His face contorted in fear.

It was Cappy, the guy who'd given me a hard time the other day when I'd been locked in the holding cell.

He leapt to his feet and clutched the bars at the front of the cell. "Hey, CO!" he called.

The CO at the desk hardly moved. "What'dya want?"

"I want out of here!"

A collective laugh went up from the inmates in the surrounding cells. An elderly, cracked voice from further on down the row shouted, "So do we all, my boy. So do we all."

"I mean it! First chance he gets, this guy's gonna hurt me! Maybe kill me!"

With a mighty sigh, the CO swung his heavy boots onto the floor and straightened his belt. He grabbed his radio and made his way down to in front of our cell.

"Now what's going on?"

"He's threatened to kill me! You need to get him out of here."

The CO peered at me. "You threaten him?" he asked.

As anyone who's ever had to appear in court without access to street clothes knows, it's not easy to look innocent when dressed in a jail jumpsuit, but I tried my best. "No, sir. I didn't say nothing at all to him."

"Make a threatening gesture?"

"No, sir."

"I can call for someone to rewind the tapes and take a look," he warned.

"Go ahead and do that, sir. I just been sitting on the bottom bunk here. He's been asleep. I haven't said a word to him."

The CO turned his attention to Cappy. "What did he say to you?"

"That I was gonna be sorry. That I'd better hope I was released before he was put in the general population."

Scratching his head under his hat, the CO said, "That doesn't make a whole lot of sense. Neither one of you is in the general population."

"I know. But he's my cell buddy now! That's even worse. All he's got to do is wait until I'm asleep, and he can strangle me."

"Weren't you just asleep now?"

"Yeah."

"And he didn't try to strangle you, did he?"

"No. But he might."

"And you might try to strangle him. What's the difference?"

Cappy looked genuinely frightened. "I'm just a two-bit minor criminal. He's a murderer. And a sex offender. And Lord knows what all else."

The CO shook his head. "Why don't you just wait until he's gone to sleep before you fall asleep yourself? Then he won't be able to strangle you."

"You're not taking this very seriously, are you?" Cappy asked.

"I'm trying to understand. He's just sitting there. I haven't heard a peep out of this cell, except for your whining."

The inmates in the surrounding cells, who had been listening intently, starting making peeping noises and laughing. The CO smiled, but Cappy just shook his head violently.

"I'm gonna sue this damn jail if anything happens to me," he said. "And sue you, too."

"Is that right?" the CO said.

"Yep."

"If he strangles you and you're dead, how can you sue anybody?"

Cappy looked confused. "My people'll sue."

"Right." The CO turned to me. "You gonna strangle him when he's asleep?"

"No, sir."

"You plan to make any threats?"

"No, sir."

From the cell next door, someone shouted, "If he don't shut up, *I'll* strangle him." A chorus of agreements chimed in.

"Do you have a keep-away order from each other?" the CO asked.

"No," Cappy conceded.

"And you're not co-defendants?"

"No."

"Then why the fuss? Just shut up and chill here."

"But I can't be locked in with him!" Cappy insisted.

"In jail, you don' get to choose who your cell buddies are."

I could attest to that. Over the last twenty years, sometimes I'd lucked out and had somebody somewhat decent, sometimes I'd been locked in with slobs or idiots or someone with a mean streak.

The CO went back to his desk. Cappy curled up on his bunk and started sobbing. Loudly. I tried to ignore him.

A little while later, the lieutenant on duty showed up. The CO must have called him. He came to the door of our cell.

"What's going on here?" he demanded.

Cappy went to the front of the cell, his eyes red. "I'm scared," he said. "This guy told me I'd better not be around where he could find me."

"Oh? And why was that?"

"I dunno."

"What did he say he was going to do?"

"Nothing specific. But he did say that he was headed to prison and didn't mind picking up some new street charges. He said if that was going to happen, he'd just as soon make it worth his while."

"What did he mean by that?"

"I think that he was gonna kill me."

"And pick up murder charges?"

"I think he's *got* murder charges now."

The lieutenant looked over at me. Once again, I tried to look as innocent as possible, despite the jail jumpsuit. "You got a problem with this guy?" he asked.

"Just that he's making a lot of noise and trying to get me in trouble," I said. "I got enough trouble as it is."

Nodding, the lieutenant said to Cappy, "Pack your stuff."

"Pack my stuff? Me? What'd I do?"

"You're creating a fuss. I'm gonna have you moved to an isolation cell."

"You're moving *me*? Why not him? *He's* the one doing the threatening."

"Not so's I've noticed. Pack your stuff up."

"Not fair."

That made me smile. If someone offered *me* an isolation cell, I'd jump at it. Especially if I was going to cry like a baby. That would offer some privacy, at least.

The lieutenant sounded like he was talking to a little kid. "It doesn't *have* to be fair. You're concerned for your safety. You got jumped down in medium security. So we moved you to a higher security level. Now you're afraid you're gonna get hurt here, too. So we'll put you in protective custody, where nobody can get to you."

"I don't *want* to go to protective custody."

"You wanna stay here with him?" The lieutenant nodded toward me.

"No. I want *him* moved."

"Not gonna happen," the lieutenant said. "Pack your stuff."

"No."

"Don't give me a rough time. Pack your stuff and let's go."

When he turned so I could see his face, his eyes were wild, and his face flushed. His breath was coming in labored gasps. "You can't make me," he said.

I cringed. Wrong thing to say to security staff in a correctional institution. In my experience, that kind of challenge brought out the macho in the staff and led to things that were never good. The lieutenant nodded to the CO assigned to the unit, who got on his radio. He was undoubtedly calling for whatever this jail used as a cell extraction team.

I could only hope the team wasn't a bunch of cowboys who relished an opportunity to use the training they got in quelling disturbances.

"Hey, can you guys get me out of here first?" I asked.

I didn't get any response from the lieutenant, who had moved away from the cell door, but Cappy moved so he was blocking the door.

"I thought you *wanted* me out of here," I said to him.

"This is all your fault. If I'm gonna get grief over this, you're gonna get some, too."

I had a feeling he didn't have any idea what he was talking about. I unsnapped my jumpsuit, pulled off my T-shirt, and redid the snaps. Then I put the shirt in the sink and ran water over it.

"What're you doing?" Cappy said, his breathing ragged and heavy.

"To cover my face," I said. "They're gonna be using pepper spray. And maybe Tasers." I hung the wet shirt on the end of my bunk. I wasn't sure I'd have time to use it, but I wanted it to be available in case they used pepper spray. I then took a wait-and-see stance.

The sound of cadenced marching boots reached us from the hallway. The cellblock door opened, and a team of five entered, all wearing body armor and each member holding onto the shirt of the person in front of him. The first in the line had a clear plastic shield.

Following the team was a CO carrying a video camera. Of course the entire procedure would be taped both to use in debriefing and training, and in case of a lawsuit. Two more came behind him, each pushing a restraint chair.

Two chairs. My heart gave a lurch. Not good. That meant they were coming after *me,* too.

All the other inmates were pressed against the fronts of their cells, watching. Glad the team wasn't coming for any of them. When the team got inside the dayroom and stopped their march, the sudden silence reverberated off the cinderblock walls of the cellblock.

The approach was by the book, designed to show discipline and intimidate the inmates. The second part, at least, worked. I didn't know about Cappy, but I was thoroughly intimidated. Maybe the team was reasonably well trained and professional. Then they would try to minimize any damage done to anyone.

When everyone was in the dayroom and the desk pushed out of the way, the lieutenant stepped up to the cell door again.

"I'm ordering you to face the back of the cell and put your hands on your head, fingers interlaced."

Cappy crossed his arms in front of his chest, a mulish expression on his face. I stepped up against the wall and complied. Facing the back of the cell, I couldn't see anything. The position would protect my eyes and nose a bit from a direct hit with the pepper spray, but the skin on my back crawled.

"If you refuse to follow orders, you will be forcibly removed from the cell. Do you understand?"

So far they were acting professionally, giving him every opportunity to avoid a showdown.

Cappy was beyond the point where he could be reasonable. I heard him move, and, without moving my feet or hands, glanced over my shoulder.

He spit through the bars at the lieutenant.

Great. Make them mad. Smart move.

"Keep looking at the back wall," the lieutenant warned me. I snapped my head back around, took a deep breath, and closed my eyes.

I heard a whooshing sound and the caustic scent of pepper spray filled the air. Although my eyes were closed and I tried to hold my breath, I felt burning in my nose and throat.

The cell door clicked open. Cappy screamed. The cell filled with flailing bodies. Five officers, each assigned to a body part. Head, left arm, right arm, left leg, right leg. One of them would be carrying restraints.

I stood unmoving, trying to keep my balance as somebody knocked into my feet.

Cappy continued to scream, partially blocking out the commands to "cease resisting and lay flat on the floor."

He was still struggling and screaming when they picked him up and carried him out of the cell.

Someone came up behind me. "I'm going to put you in restraints. Don't resist." It was a woman's voice. *They had a woman on their cell extraction team?* Some of the best CO's I known had been women, so I guess it shouldn't have been a surprise. And they tried to have at least one small person on the team. A small person could move around easier in the limited space of a cell and was often the one who handled the restraints.

I didn't resist as she took one of my hands and maneuvered it behind me, turning the palm out, and locked a cuff on the wrist, tighter than necessary. The other hand followed. Then she knelt and snapped a leg cuff around each ankle. I didn't turn to look, but I knew there was at least one other another person behind me ready to intervene if I tried to kick or something.

She grabbed my arm and turned me around.

Cappy was still struggling as they strapped him into the restraint chair, a spit shield strapped over his face. The cameraman was sweeping back and forth between him and me.

Someone else took my other arm and the two CO's guided me out of the cell. My eyes were watering, and I was having trouble seeing. I almost tripped over the plastic shield which had been discarded right outside the cell door.

I'd lost my shower shoes somewhere along the line. The concrete floor was cold on my bare feet. I shivered.

"Put this one in a chair, too?" one of the team, his face invisible behind the face shield on his helmet, asked the lieutenant.

Please, no. "I'm cooperating," I said. I wiped my eyes as best I could on the shoulder of my jumpsuit. The non-absorbent fabric felt scratchy.

Cappy's screams were muted by the spit shield they'd put over his face. He struggled against the chair's straps as they were tightened.

The lieutenant looked at me. "Are you gonna comply with orders?"

"Yes, sir." My voice was raspy, and I coughed.

"Just hold him here until we get the other one down to medical," he said. "He'll need to be looked at, too."

"But do you want him in the chair?"

Much to my relief, the lieutenant shook his head. "He's been compliant. I think he'll be all right shackled up like that."

The hallway door to the cellblock slid open, and several members of the team left, pushing Cappy ahead of them on the restraint chair. His screams echoed down the hall.

I tried to wipe my eyes again. "There's a wet T-shirt on the end of my bunk," I said to the woman who was still holding my arm. "Do you think you could wipe my face with it?"

She looked at the lieutenant, who nodded and came over to hold the arm she released. She came back with the shirt and held it up to my face. It didn't completely relief the burning, but it felt a lot better.

"You been through this before, I take it?" the lieutenant asked me.

"A few times. I got a knack of having cell buddies who decide they're gonna make an issue of something stupid."

"You spend a lot of time locked up?"

I shrugged. "Twenty years. So far." I was looking at a lot more than that now.

CHAPTER 14

A few hours later, I was back in the cell, alone. The nurse did the best he could washing out my eyes and checking my breathing. I could still feel the burning, especially in my throat and lungs, but he assured me there was no lasting damage done. My wrists were bruised and sore where the cuffs had been clamped down too tightly, but there wasn't much to be done for that.

While I had been gone, someone had packed up Cappy's things and moved them. I sat on one of the bottom bunks and pulled out my charging papers to read them again. The words made my chest tighten up again. Rehashing this was just going to drive me even crazier. I needed something to distract me.

I folded the papers, put them down and went to door. "Hey, CO!" I called.

Although he didn't move, his response was instantaneous. "What?"

"Can you get me something to read?"

He stirred. "Not right now. When I go on break, I'll see if I can stop by the library and get you a book. What d'ya want?"

Smart guy. He realized that an inmate who is reading is going to be easier to handle. Calmer, less likely to be a behavior problem, and not as inclined to think up more problematic ways to pass the time.

I said, "I don't care. History, maybe. Or a novel. But make it a long one."

"Okay. I got a newspaper here. You wanna look at that for now?"

"Yes, please."

He swung his feet off the desk and opened a drawer. Pulling out a newspaper, he came over and handed it through the bars, careful to stay far enough back that I couldn't have grabbed him if I'd wanted to.

I took it. "Thanks."

The front page had a big picture of the bridge construction site. The story underneath took up most of the bottom of the page. The headline read, "Body Uncovered at Construction Site."

I had a pretty good idea whose body it was.

The article, written by one Carissa Daniles, described how a Transportation Construction Inspector had shown up for work and discovered the site didn't meet specifications. She was quoted as saying that the silt snakes that controlled erosion were misaligned and the drainage was all wrong, and that construction could not continue until it was fixed.

According to the article, the foreman insisted that his workers had left the site as the inspector had approved it just the afternoon before when they quit work, but he had no practical choice but to comply with the TCI's instructions. At that point, several day workers, who would not be paid while the work was stopped, became angry and left the site.

Under the inspector's supervision, the remaining workers, including a heavy equipment operator, set about moving the silt snakes and resloping the site.

As the backhoe removed soil from a pile, buried bits of cloth became visible. The foreman waved the backhoe off and grabbed a shovel. A little digging uncovered a human arm.

The construction site became a crime scene.

The body, a white male in his thirties, had not yet been identified. The cause of death appeared to be blunt force trauma, but official results would not be released until after an autopsy. The police were investigating—no surprise there. At press time the police were seeking several "people of interest," including the workers who had left the site.

Although the article didn't say so, I must have been a "person of interest." And they'd found me.

I read the entire paper, including the classified ads. It distracted me a bit, and I could fight down the panic in my chest.

Ever since my release from prison, I'd lived with the constant possibility that I'd be returning to prison. It was part of the parole experience, especially for anyone convicted of a violent crime. No matter how hard I tried to comply with the parole restrictions and follow the rules, I had to admit being locked up again was coming as no real surprise. Had I really expected to be able to live for the next twenty years or so without being sent back to prison? A very depressing thought, but I had to admit it was highly unlikely.

Of course, if I was honest with myself, I'd have to admit I'd been taking a few unwise chances in the past few days.

The CO brought me back a mega novel by Ken Follett that I hadn't read yet. I took it gratefully and wrapped myself in my blanket, settling in to read. Anything to take my mind off my less than promising situation. And Kelly. Who I would probably never see again in this lifetime.

Even after the official lights out, I could see pretty well by the security light, and I read until I fell asleep.

* * * *

Breakfast came early. It was those rehydrated dried egg squares again. Not bad, but not enough to fill me. The CO supervised the inmate kitchen worker closely, and when they came around to collect the tray, I put down the book and asked, "You got a newspaper I can look at?"

The CO looked at me, then grinned. "Wanna see yourself on the front page, do you?"

I was afraid of that.

"We only get the one paper for the whole unit," he said as he handed it to me. "So don't go doing the Sudoku or the crossword on the newspaper," he said. "If you want to do them, trace them and leave the one in the paper so other people can do them, too."

"I don't got any paper," I pointed out. "Or anything to write with. But I'll be careful with the paper. I just want to read it."

He grinned again. "Lousy picture of you, I got to say."

I thought it was going to be the mug shot from my booking, but Carissa had resurrected the picture of me being hauled in last week, all bruised up and looking like a total maniac. *Thoughtful of her, that was.*

She recapped my original conviction. Then she went into Kelly's rape, although she once again primly noted the *Rothsburg Register* policy about victims of sexual assaults, so referred to her as "the victim." The article said I'd originally been a suspect in that but been cleared by DNA evidence. That was news to me. Now, she said, I had been arrested for the murder of the alleged assailant, and speculated on the relationships among me, "the victim," and Razorback, who she identified as Harvey McGillian.

Since I already had one murder conviction and this charge was premeditated first degree murder with aggravating circumstances, the state's attorney was contemplating filing the paperwork to make it a capital case.

Great. Although I was well aware of the possibility of a death sentence, and it was mentioned in the charging papers, reading about it in a newspaper in connection with my name sent a chill down my spine.

Remembering how everybody at work had seen the last article, I figured they would all see this one, too.

So what? I tried to tell myself that it didn't matter, I didn't care what they thought anyhow. But I did. It had been the first time in my life I'd had a "normal" job. With a potential future.

Kelly probably wouldn't have much to say about me at work, and nobody else would be likely to ask unless she brought it up. She'd probably be mad. Or worse, now that I seemed to be on a fast track back to prison, she'd pity me.

To me, the article seemed biased. Since when did newspapers let ditzy feature writers present what should have been a news article? But there it was, with Carissa's byline and everything. And I had to admit I wasn't exactly an objective reader.

"Damon. Somebody to see you," the CO called from his seat at the desk. "Bring your ID."

I slipped the square of toilet paper I was using for a bookmark between the pages of the book and sat up, feeling around on the floor for the shower shoes. I folded the newspaper to give back to the CO. Maybe I'd finally been assigned an attorney.

With the possibility of this being a capital case, they'd have to assign somebody halfway decent, wouldn't they? I hoped. There'd be lots of public scrutiny in the press and such. But if most of it came through Carissa, I had my doubts about the reporting.

An experienced public defender might be my best bet, although I couldn't imagine they'd have one who would be willing to fight the murder charges. Just get the best deal possible. Like life with the possibility of parole. I'd never get another shot at parole, though. Not if I picked up another murder conviction.

I put those depressing thoughts out of my mind, brushed my hair back, and snapped up the jumpsuit. The hallway door to the cellblock slid open, and a CO came in and up to my cell, radioing a request to pop the door. I stepped out. He checked my ID band, then moved aside so I could shuffle off ahead of him.

He didn't have to answer me, but I asked, "Lawyer?"

Frowning, he said, "I dunno. I didn't recognize him. Looked like a lawyer, though. But not a public defender. Black guy. Spiffy dresser. And not in a harried mood."

That was encouraging. Maybe they'd assigned a private lawyer who would take a real interest in the case, even if he was just getting whatever it was that the county paid per hour for attorneys. Nothing like what they were used to making. But it wasn't unheard of to get enthusiastic representation from an interested private attorney.

We arrived at the meeting room where I'd previously talked with Montgomery. The door slid open, and I entered. No one was waiting. I looked back at the CO, but he just waved me in.

I sat in one of the cushioned chairs and looked around. I couldn't be sure, but I'd bet there was a camera behind the dark window and my every move was being watched. I sat down and closed my eyes.

A little while later the door on the opposite side of the room opened. Montgomery came in. Not a lawyer. I wasn't sure whether this was a good development or not. At least he didn't have Belkins along.

He slid into the chair on the opposite side of the table. I nodded a greeting.

"So," he said, straightening the crease in his trousers, "how are things going?"

I hated it when he asked things like that. "I'm locked up on a new murder charge. I'll be lucky to get out of this with a life sentence. How the hell do you *think* I'm doing?"

He shook his head. "I guess when you put it like that, not well. I got a few questions to ask you."

"I don't got many answers."

"Let's try anyhow. How well did you know Razorback?"

"Not at all. I wouldn't have recognized him if I'd tripped over him."

"But you know some of the Predators."

"Not really. Old Buckles was a commissary clerk at the prison, so I knew who he was. Everybody knew him."

"And the others?"

"If I ever met any of them, it was in prison. And they certainly weren't wearing club colors with their state-issue denims, so I have no idea if I've met any of them."

"Wasn't there a little altercation outside the hospital?"

Of course he'd heard about that. "With Funky Joe? Yeah."

"And just after I'd told you to stay away from there."

I didn't answer that one.

"Am I right?" he asked.

"Yeah."

He stood up and walked behind me. "You knew about the chop shop at the clubhouse?"

"I was only out there the once. They were working on cars and it certainly looked like a chop shop, but what do I know about that crap? I don't even have a driver's license."

"And were they running a meth lab?"

"That I don't know. There was kind of an ammonia smell, so I thought maybe they were, but I didn't see anything. If they were, it was probably one of those little shake-and-bake ones with the plastic soda bottles."

He paced behind me. "We used some pictures that woman reporter took on her cell phone up there to get a warrant. By the time we got up there, any traces of a clandestine lab were gone."

I couldn't figure out where this was taking us, so I kept quiet. Reporting my noncooperation to Mr. Ramirez at this point didn't seem like a big deal.

"Same reporter who got the pictures of you with the Predators in the park."

I shrugged. "Yeah, well, what can I say?"

"Not a whole hell of a lot. We have the pictures. You gonna tell me about Black Rose?"

"What about her?"

"She talked a lot about you."

"I can't help that."

"She's quite a woman. You know she and Razorback ran a business together?"

"Yeah. A trenching and excavating business. The clubhouse was in a big garage on the same property."

"That's right." He leaned forward. "Did you know Black Rose did most of the work for the business? Operated the backhoe and kept the books."

"I knew she handled the backhoe." That didn't seem particularly surprising to me. Women did all kinds of jobs these days. After all, Kelly drove a forklift. "And I'm not surprised she kept the books. I wouldn't have trusted any of the Predators to keep *my* books. Not if I didn't want all the profits to disappear."

"When Razorback decided to take off, he cleaned out the business's bank account. They'd been saving for some more equipment, so there was a fair amount in there."

"I bet Black Rose wasn't happy about that."

"You're right about that." He leaned back in his chair. "Do you know how to operate a backhoe?"

"I haven't ever. I've never really taken a look at the controls. I'd think it'd be pretty complicated."

"More complicated than the forklift you drive at work?"

"Got to be. It's got more variables."

"Think you could learn to operate it?"

"I suppose, given some instruction and a little time."

Montgomery pulled a small notebook from the inner pocket of his suit jacket and consulted it. "What I don't understand is why you have such a different story from what Black Rose says."

"What does Black Rose say?"

"Well, you know the whole bit about how she says you and Razorback agreed to swap women. She said you took full advantage of it. And that she liked it fine. But you never said anything to Kelly, and she got a raw deal."

"That's because it never happened. Black Rose saying it doesn't make it true."

Montgomery glanced up at me and then back at his notebook. "When Kelly was hurt badly enough that she got sent to the hospital, Razorback knew he was likely to be in trouble. Especially since he's already a registered sex offender. So he decided to take the money out of the bank and lie low."

"Yeah."

"But Razorback was mad. He blamed you. And he didn't like that Black Rose was telling everybody what a good lay you gave her."

I shrugged.

"I'm trying to put together what happened. At first I thought you and Black Rose decided to off Razorback and get together. But why would you deny everything, especially if Black Rose was busy bragging about it? Something's wrong with that theory."

There was plenty wrong with that theory, but I had no answer for him that I thought he might be willing to listen to.

He changed tactics. "The coroner places Razorback's death sometime before noon last Saturday."

"You had me locked up on Saturday. I didn't get sprung until late afternoon."

"And the bank has a video of Razorback withdrawing all that money from a couple of ATMs. The last one was about ten o'clock Friday night."

I sat up. "I was locked up then, too. That means…"

"That means for the murder itself, you have as ironclad an alibi for the time of Razorback's death as it's possible to have."

The muscles in my back and neck tightened further. Had I heard right? "So I *can't* have been the one who killed Razorback. And they'll have to drop the murder charges."

He nodded.

I felt the muscle tightness begin to relax a bit. I hadn't fully appreciated just how tense my body had been holding itself.

"That's true. But don't forget there's still the possibility of accessory charges. And conspiracy."

Not a great prospect. But at least they probably wouldn't carry a death penalty.

I had to wonder, though, if a death penalty wouldn't beat growing old and dying in prison.

CHAPTER 15

When I had another court hearing the next morning, via video conference from the jail, those charges were dropped without prejudice. Which meant they could be reinstated at any time.

But at least I got out of jail.

I had a few days before I had to make my parole appointment. If Mr. Ramirez had been unhappy with me last time, I could just imagine what he'd have to say this time. Or what he'd decide to do. My ankle itched where a monitoring box would be strapped on if he decided I needed more supervision. And that might be one of the least restrictive of the measures he would consider.

Since the plant was mostly shut down for retooling and they hadn't told me to report, I had plenty of time. If I could figure out what had happened to Razorback, I could contact Montgomery. He'd listen to me. But I'd need some real facts, not just theories.

Sounded like they'd busted the chop shop up at the clubhouse. It hadn't been in the newspapers I'd read in the jail, and I'd read every word in them, front to back. Maybe it would be in today's paper. I could go buy a copy, or I could go up to the library to read their copy.

The library was a better option. I could look for a copy of the Ken Follet book. I'd only gotten a third into it read while I was locked up. And if all the copies were out, I could put in a request for them to hold one for me.

I stopped by my apartment to pick up the library books that were due.

A few things caught my eye immediately. The ice cube trays were in the sink, empty. The box that had held biscuit mix was in the trash, empty. And floury traces of the mix were on the kitchen counter.

My apartment had been searched. Thoroughly. Probably by cops—it wasn't all torn up, and things were left more or less neatly stacked. But no effort had been made to hide the fact that it had been searched.

Since I was on parole, they had the right to search it any time they wanted. I didn't keep anything at all that could get me in trouble. No drugs, no weapons, no alcohol. It still felt like an invasion of my space and a reminder that I had no right to expect privacy or the other rights most people took for granted as long as I was on parole. At least I hadn't had to stand and watch, the way I had to do in prison whenever my cell was shaken down.

I checked my little stash of cash. I'd only been able to save just under a hundred dollars, but it had taken me weeks. I left it rolled inside a pair of socks in a drawer of my rickety dresser.

The socks were unrolled, but to my relief, the cash was still there.

And confirmed that it had been police who had conducted the search.

I was glad the cat and her kittens hadn't been there—I knew of any number of instances where doors had been left open during a search and pets had run out. I wondered how they were making out at Kelly's place.

Picking up the library books, I headed back out.

Mandy was helping somebody else, so I went back in the stacks to see if I could find another copy of the book I'd been reading. I couldn't find one. I went over to the comfortable chairs that surrounded a table with newspapers and magazines. The last few days worth of the *Rothsburg Register* were laid out on the table in a pile. I took the most recent one.

Carissa had gotten a front page story again. There was a brief factual article about a raid on a garage back in the hills that uncovered an operation where stolen cars were disassembled for parts. It was on the same grounds as a company called General Trench and Excavating, but there was no apparent connection. It listed the names of a few people arrested, but since I was familiar with only a few of the Predators, and then only by street names, I couldn't tell if I knew any of them.

Under the fold, Carissa had a big feature article and an array of pictures she'd taken up at the clubhouse. She wrote about how her investigative reporting had led her to the site, where she had taken the photographs that enabled the police to get a search warrant. Neither article made mention of the Predators or that Carissa's intended project had been about a motorcycle gang. Or how close she'd come to being the victim of a gang rape. Or worse, if they would've decided not to leave a living victim who might get them in trouble.

The articles did let me know that the chop shop was out of operation, at least for the time being, but it didn't supply many details. I refolded the paper and put it back on the pile.

With the most recent edition of the paper in my hand, yesterday's was on top. I'd forgotten that my picture graced the front page of that one. There I was, looking dangerous and disreputable, but still recognizably me.

A woman who was sitting across the table put down her magazine and looked at the paper. Then she looked at me. And back at the paper. A look of alarm came over her face. She hurriedly gathered her things, got to her feet and headed toward the children's section of the library.

Mandy was sorting books behind the counter when I went up. She turned and smiled as she filled in the information about the book I wanted. "You'll get a phone call when it's available," she said.

"Did they ever find your car?" I asked her.

She grimaced. "Yes. But it wasn't much help. They just called yesterday to tell me they found *pieces* of it. Looks like someone stole for parts and there's not a whole lot left."

"I'm sorry to hear that," I said, thinking what a loss it must be, even if it was insured. The insurance *never* paid enough to replace a reliable car.

She shrugged. "I got a new one. A convertible! It's a lot more fun than that stodgy old Mercedes. If I'd gotten that back, I'd probably just have gotten rid of it anyhow."

It had been, what, two years old? Mandy lived in a different financial world than I did.

A few blocks away from the library, I heard the throaty roar of motorcycles before I saw them. Four bikes jumped the curb, surrounding me on the sidewalk. I stopped walking and backed up so a brick wall was at my back.

Funky Joe, a mean smirk on his face, got off his bike. The others straddled theirs.

"Going somewhere?" Funky Joe leered at me, baring his broken and rotten teeth. He made a fist with his right hand and slapped it into his left palm.

Don't show fear. I kept my eyes steady. "Home," I said. "A few nights in jail is enough to make you appreciate it."

The other two guys I could see nodded understandingly.

"Got somebody who wants to see you," he said, taking a step toward me.

"Yeah? Anybody I know?"

"I think so. Old Buckles."

"It's not hard to find me. He can see me any time he wants to."

"*Now* might be a good time."

Didn't look like I was going to have much choice in this, so I might as well maintain what dignity and control I could. "Now would suit me fine. Do you know where he is?"

"Yeah. In fact, we've come to take you to him."

"Okay. Somebody giving me a ride or am I walking?"

Funky Joe reached into his pocket. "You're coming with us."

"That sounds like a plan," I said. *What was he reaching for?*

He pulled out a big knife and some rope. Then he turned to the others, who were still straddling their bikes. "You guys gonna give me a hand here?"

They didn't move.

Funky Joe looked back at them, his eyes dark. "I said, you guys gonna give me a hand here?"

The biker on the left leaned back in his seat. "Don't look to me like you need a whole lot of help," he said. "Guy says he's gonna come along. You don't need to tie him up or nothing."

"What kind of wusses are you?" Funky Joe practically shouted. "He's just one guy. Come help me with this."

No one moved.

Finally I said, "I'd rather one of you other guys told me where to find Old Buckles. Or gave me a ride. Don't look to me like I want to be riding with Funky Joe."

The same guy on the left nodded and inched forward in his seat. "Get up behind me," he said.

Without taking my eyes off Funky Joe, I went over and swung my leg over the saddle on his bike, settling in behind him.

"You ride on a bike before?" he asked.

"Nope," I said. Another of the many things experiences prison didn't offer.

"Just hang onto me and lean the same way I do, and we'll be fine."

We roared away. The two-wheeler was nothing like the trike I'd been on with Old Buckles. I could feel the throbbing power of the engine between my thighs.

The midday traffic wasn't heavy, but most of the drivers made way for us. We skimmed through stop signs and traffic lights, took corners leaning close to the pavement, and ignored speed limits.

This was heady stuff. I could understand why people would gravitate to a lifestyle like this. Especially if they had never been able to achieve respect in their lives for anything else.

We made our way through a long alley, emerging in a truck yard in front of a warehouse. It looked abandoned, with rusted, discarded parts piled randomly on the blacktop and trash blowing up against the chain-link fence.

One garage door stood partway open, and the bikes slid through it, skidding to a stop in the center of the floor. Several other bikes, including Old Buckles' trike, were parked along a wall.

We dismounted and stood around. The bikers pulled out smokes. Funky Joe went through an office door and emerged a few minutes later. "Old Buckles wants to see you now," he said, grabbing my arm.

I was accustomed to being escorted by police and correctional officers, but a biker? I shrugged my arm loose and said, "Let's not tear the jacket, shall we? It may not be much, but it's all I've got."

The biker I'd been riding behind guffawed.

Funky Joe scowled and grabbed my arm again, more tightly this time. I yanked my arm free. He reached into his pocket and pulled out a knife.

Everyone else backed up and formed a circle around us.

I went into a crouch to provide a smaller target and edged away to the left.

Funky Joe followed me, the knife in his hand, the blade picking up the dim rays of light filtering through the high dusty windows.

What would happen if I managed to knock the knife out of Funky Joe's hand? Would all the bikers join in and tackle me?

I'd just have to take that chance. I watched for an opening, holding my right hand forward and poised so he would think I was planning to make a grab for his wrist with it. I continued to move to the left, backing slowly away from him. Funky Joe kept step with me, his eyes staring into mine.

The circle of bikers moved with us.

Boot steps sounded on the concrete floor from behind me. I couldn't afford to stop focusing on the knife to see what was going on, so I ignored them.

Funky Joe glanced up.

As soon as he'd broken eye contact, I aimed a kick at his lower arm. The wrist and the knife were too small a target, too easy to miss. I was wearing the only footwear I owned, the steel-toed work boots. They were clumsy, but they made an effective weapon.

As my boot hit, he cried out and grabbed at his arm. The knife flew across the garage, clattering as it hit the floor.

Tucking my head down, I launched myself at him, butting him in the gut and knocking him to the floor. I collapsed on top of him, wrapping my arms around his chest and trying to keep his hands tucked between us and my weight to keep him down.

I hoped no one else would join in. If it was just the two of us, I stood a good chance, but no way could I hold my own against the entire group.

Someone grabbed me by the neck of the jacket and yanked me upward. Somebody else grabbed my arms and pulled them back behind me, holding me with my elbows immobile behind me. With my legs trailing behind me, I couldn't get my feet under me and if they'd let go, I would have fallen to the floor.

All I could hear was my own labored breathing. I ducked my head and closed my eyes, bracing myself against the first blow.

When a few seconds went by and it didn't come, I chanced a glance around.

Across the open space, a few other bikers had Funky Joe in the same position. He was struggling with them. "Ouch!" he cried. "Let go! He broke my arm! And you're making it worse!"

I got my feet under me and stood on my own, letting the bikers continue to hold my elbows. Their grip relaxed, but not enough for me to try to pull away.

One of the guys bent down and picked up the knife from the floor, pocketing it. Funky Joe continued to whine about his arm being broken.

From somewhere behind me, Old Buckles stepped up between us. He gestured at me. "Take him into my office."

The bikers looked puzzled. Old Buckles grinned. "I've always wanted to be able to say that," he said. "Ever since I got in trouble with the principal for fighting in school. That's what he used to say. But take him into that back room anyhow."

"I can walk on my own, thanks," I said, shaking loose from the hands that were holding me. I straightened my jacket and followed Old Buckles through the doorway.

"I'm still trying to puzzle this whole thing out." Old Buckles perched his massive rear end on a dusty table. "And where you fit into it."

I just shook my head.

"Before I was even released from prison, Kelly was talking about you. A lot. She seemed to really like you. Did you know that?"

"Well, I really like her. And she was awful nice to me."

"I told her you'd been locked up for a long time. Ever since you were a kid. So she should be careful—who could tell how being out on the street was going to hit you? Maybe after a little while the novelty would wear off, and you'd revert to the kind of behavior that got you locked up to begin with."

"Like you say, I was a just kid then. Never really got a chance to get too involved in much before I got locked up."

He nodded. "So I told her you were an unknown."

"That was fair enough."

"I did tell her you weren't one of them braggarts or somebody who was involved in all kinds of shit in prison. Worked your job in the laundry, kept your nose clean, went along with the official agenda."

"Just trying to make my time as easy as possible."

"When I found out she was seeing you, I asked around some. Found out you weren't one of them that goes in for sex with whatever's available. Pretty much kept to yourself."

He was right, but not much to say to that.

"So I didn't expect it when Black Rose started talking about the deal you and Razorback made. Didn't make sense to me."

"That's 'cause there never was a deal."

"I get that now. But why would Black Rose make all that up?"

"Maybe to cover for Razorback? I figured if she spread that story, a lot of people would think it was an agreement gone wrong, not Razorback attacking Kelly for no reason other than that he wanted to screw her. Kind of puts a different perspective on the whole thing."

"Yeah. I finally decided that might be it. Razorback wasn't used to women who'd try to fight him off. I mean, even if a woman said no, she'd be likely to give in when he overpowered her. Happens all the time with the guys. The women who hang around know that. Otherwise they should stay away."

"Don't work like that with Kelly. Especially in her own house."

Old Buckles smiled. "You're right on that. My little girl don't take kindly to nobody messing with her." He shifted his weight. "And it don't take into account that Razorback had to know damn well a registered sex offender wasn't going to get away with it."

I considered. "Maybe he figured Kelly would never report it to the cops. Just keep it in the club."

"Yeah, maybe. But she was hurt too bad to not go to the emergency room. Stupid of him. But then, you don't get to be a registered sex offender by showing a whole lot of restraint."

"True, that."

Old Buckles fingered his beard. "I feel a bit responsible. I mean, she let me use her address for a home plan. Fine. But then I let some of the Predators hang around. That wasn't part of the deal. She didn't like it."

"Were you on home detention, with an ankle monitor and all?"

He gave a dismissive wave of his hand. "Nah. Nothing like that."

"Then why were you at her place so much? Especially with other people?"

"Did you know what was going on up at the clubhouse?"

I closed my eyes and pictured the scene. "You mean the chop shop? Or the meth lab?"

He laughed. "You knew about all that, huh? Not as dumb as some of the guys think you are. But it was mostly the chop shop. I knew my PO was going to be checking up on me. And while this time I was locked up for fighting, I got a few car theft convictions in the past. Wouldn't want have that brought up again."

"So you just tried to stay away?"

"Yeah. Figured I'd be released from supervision in a few months. Then I could go where I pleased. Until then, I could be careful."

"Even if it meant causing problems for Kelly."

"Well, I didn't know it was gonna cause all *those* problems. I mean, I was planning to pay some rent and maybe get to know my grandkids a bit."

I tried to get back to my main concern. "You think you know happened to Razorback?"

He raised his bushy eyebrows and stroked his braided beard. "Oh, I *know* what happened to Razorback."

"Yeah?"

"And I didn't have nothing to do with it. Mind you, if I'd had a chance, I might have."

"And?"

"Come to find out, you didn't have nothing to do with it, either. I thought maybe you did—I see the way you handle yourself with Funky Joe when he's getting a bit too big for his britches. And they say the first killing's the hardest one. You got that one under your belt. So you might think knocking off Razorback would be more of a 'could-you-get-away-with-it' kind of thing."

"But I didn't."

"I know. It was Black Rose."

"Really? I thought she might be involved somehow, but why'd she want to off her old man? I mean, it didn't bother her that much that he had the hots for Kelly, did it?"

"Nah. That was no big deal. But when he realized Kelly was in the hospital and there was probably no way he was gonna avoid street charges, he decided to take off."

"I know Kelly was plenty mad, but I'm not at all sure she'd testify against him. Might just let you take care of it."

"You know, they got those domestic abuse laws now, look into it even if the victim says she doesn't want to prosecute. And they didn't know who it was attacked her at first. Thought it might be you. So they took the swabs, ran the tests."

"And got a match with a registered sex offender."

"Yeah."

"Well, now there's nothing for anybody to do about it. Nothing anybody *can* do about it. He's dead." He nodded. "Taken care of for me. For Kelly, too. And you."

I'd heard about the money angle, but that didn't seem like reason enough to make her so mad she'd *kill* him. "So why'd Black Rose get so bent out of shape that she did him in?"

Old Buckles leaned back. "Remember he decided to take off, without her. And to finance it, he decided to take all their money out of the bank. Black Rose had worked hard for that money. She wasn't about to let it go for something stupid. So when she confronted him and he wouldn't give it back to her, she killed him."

"How'd she do that?"

"Knocked him out with a crowbar and then ran him over with the backhoe. He's got tread-marks on his head and ass."

"Then she buried him at the construction site?"

"Yeah. Stupid bitch. She had the backhoe, so it wasn't that hard. But she didn't know about how fussy they were about the slopes and the hills and all that stuff."

"Is that why the inspector said they had to fix the drainage?"

"Yeah. When the TCI came and took a look, she knew there was something wrong. Even I could tell the silt snakes weren't in the right place. She made the foreman get to work fixing it before we could get to work."

"That can't have gone over well."

"Nope. Most of us couldn't work until they got it fixed. And then when they found out what happened, most of us lost our jobs. Go figure."

"So what happens now?"

Old Buckles reached into his pocket and pulled out a keychain with a few keys dangling from it. He held it up and then tossed in my direction.

"Here. Go by the house and take care of the cats. Kelly's in the rehab place. She'll be pissed if she finds out anything happened to the damn things."

I caught it. "Where are you gonna be?"

He shrugged his massive shoulders. "Out riding somewhere. Until they pick me up."

"The cops?"

"I'm sure there's gonna be a retake warrant for parole violation."

"I thought you stayed away from the chop shop. And the meth lab."

"Yeah. But there was a party last night, in that roadhouse out by where the bridge is being built. I should have stayed away."

"You get drunk and do something?"

"You might say. There was a fight. A good old-fashioned brawl. That stupid bitch of yours from the newspaper took lots of pictures. Gonna put me right in the middle of the mix."

"Bitch of *mine*?"

"Yeah, well, maybe not yours. But if you hadn't gotten her out of the clubhouse, she wouldn't have been in any shape to take pictures at that bar."

"If I hadn't and you'd gone up there, you and a bunch of the Predators might have been looking at some pretty serious charges instead of a retake warrant."

"Sometimes it's worth it."

"Not if it means you're gonna spend the next few decades locked up."

He flipped his beard with his fingers. "You know, if you hadn't stepped in, there's a very good chance nobody would ever have found that bitch. Or figured out what happened to her."

"Too many people knew she was looking to go to the clubhouse. Including one guy none of you guys were smart enough to figure out is a snitch."

"Yeah? Who's that?"

"I ain't giving no names. But if anybody thinks about it, it ought to be pretty obvious."

Old Buckles nodded. "Yeah. I think I know who you mean."

"Where you gonna go?"

"Don't matter much. See what I can see before I get locked up again."

I found that plan—or lack thereof—to be a chilling thought. "That what you really want to do?"

He nodded. "Just make sure them cats get fed or whatever. I promised Kelly I'd make sure they wasn't forgot. If she gets mad at me, she won't come visit. Or send any money in or anything else. She's the only one I can really count on."

"Nobody left at the house now?"

"Shouldn't be. Now that the chop shop operation's out of the clubhouse, I imagine everybody's moved back there. I don't know how long I got here, but I'm gonna make the most of it."

"I'll go take care of the cats. But I need to be gone before Kelly gets there."

He shifted his weight from one massive leg to the other and looked past me. "Maybe you could clean up some, too. She's not gonna like what she sees. I think she just went to that rehab place today. Not drug rehab, for her shoulder. Ought to be a few days at least."

I sighed. "How bad a mess is it?"

"Not too bad. Not much furniture broken up or anything. You ought to go see Kelly again, anyhow. In the rehab place."

"She don't want to see me."

"I think she knows by now that you didn't screw Black Rose. Or tell Razorback he could screw her. So even if she's still a little mad at you, she'll get over it."

I wasn't so sure. The sharp pain that I'd been getting whenever I thought about her had turned into a pretty constant dull ache. Even if she did get over it, I wasn't so sure I'd be able to trust her again. What kind of a relationship could I have with someone I couldn't trust?

We walked out into the garage. The door was wide open now. A few of the bikers hung around, smoking those Roll-Rites that smelled of tobacco and marijuana.

Funky Joe was gone. So was his bike.

Old Buckles climbed on his trike. It sank a few inches under his weight.

"I'm going on a *run*," he announced to the others. "Ain't been on a proper run in years. Anybody coming with me?"

One of the bikers flicked the end of his smoke across the room and headed for his bike. "Where to?"

"I don't know, and I don't care. As long and as far as I can go. Until they catch up with me." He revved his engine and turned back to me. "Tell Kelly she'll probably have to arrange to have my trike picked up from where ever. Don't want it sitting in an impound lot out in the weather. And racking up fees I can't pay. She can store it in her garage again for me. Tell her thanks."

I didn't tell him I doubted I'd be seeing Kelly again, except maybe at work. No way to avoid that. But I could leave her a note.

"You want a ride over to the house?" he asked me.

"No thanks. I'll walk." It was a hike, but breathing the fresh air would do me some good. And let me think about things a little.

He raised his feet to the footrests, gunned the engine and took off, skidding through the open door and down the alley. A few of the bikers followed him.

I watched him go. I wondered if all he was worried about was parole violation from a rowdy party at a bar. Despite what he said, he might be looking at something more serious. Like having a hand in Razorback's death. I pocketed the keychain and set out toward Kelly's house across town.

As I emerged from the alley, I saw the puke-green car parked on the street. I turned to go the other way. Too late. Carissa and her camera had caught me. Probably along with Funky Joe when he left. And Old Buckles. Once again, she'd caught me where I shouldn't be.

"Hey, Jesse," she said, lowering the camera. She'd regained her spunk and didn't seem much the worse for wear. Makeup did a good job of covering the bruises on her face. If I hadn't known they were there, I wouldn't have noticed them.

"I'm still working on my feature article about the Predators," she said. "I wanted to ask you, why don't you wear a jacket with a patch and ride a motorcycle like the rest of them?"

"Because I'm not a member," I reminded her. "And I don't *want* to be a member." I also don't have a driver's license and wasn't about to waste money on a bike, even if I could afford it, but I didn't go into all that.

"You really expect me to believe that? All the time you hang around with them?"

"They're nobody to be hanging around, Carissa. I try to avoid them when I can. After the problems you've had with them, don't you think you should be, too?"

She tossed her once-again perfectly coifed blond hair and laughed. "I've got a new boyfriend," she said. "He'll make sure I don't have any more problems."

The passenger side door of the hybrid opened. Belkins lumbered out. "He giving you a hard time, pumpkin?" he said to Carissa.

CHAPTER 16

Cold rain began to slash at me as I walked. I shoved my hands in my pockets and wondered what I should do. Take the mother cat and her two kittens back to my place? That'd be a hell of a lot easier than walking to Kelly's house a couple of times a day to check on them, put out food and clean the litter box.

Kelly was in the physical rehab place, but I had no idea for how long. She'd hate staying there. Since it was just her shoulder, she could probably get around okay, and once they showed her the exercises or whatever she was supposed to do, she'd be chomping at the bit to come home and reclaim her house and kids.

How were the kids doing? Aunt Louise would make sure they were well cared for, but they were scared and worried about their mom. With good reason.

And aside from the fact that I'd agreed to take care of the cats, how was this any of my business?

The house was dark when I got there. At least there were no bikes in the driveway or on the lawn. It wasn't an expensive neighborhood, but it was quiet and well-kept, so I imagined the neighbors would be relieved if the bikers didn't come around anymore.

I went up on the porch and fit the key in the lock. As soon as the door swung open, I could smell the cat litter pan. And stale beer. With a faint undertone of marijuana.

At least the cats still seemed to be there. And alive.

The living room was a mess. Beer bottles, empty pizza boxes, all kinds of trash was strewn all over the furniture and the floor.

Stepping over everything, I went to the kitchen where the big bag of cat food had been propped in a corner next to the refrigerator. Sure enough, it was spilled out over the floor. So at least they hadn't starved.

The kitchen wasn't in any better shape than the living room. Dirty dishes and glasses filled the sink and the table. Unwashed pots were stacked on the stovetop.

Taking two cans of cat food from the pantry shelf, I looked around for the feeding bowls. They were nowhere to be seen. I looked up in the cabinet where Kelly kept bowls for soup and cereal. Empty.

Kelly shouldn't have to come home to this mess. Especially with a bad shoulder.

So why should I care? It didn't look like Kelly and I had much of a future. But much as tried to convince myself I really didn't care, my gut told me I did. It wouldn't change anything between us if I cleaned up some, but it wouldn't hurt. And it would make things a little easier on Kelly when she got back.

With a sigh, I went to the sink and started sorting out the dishes. When I'd filled the dishwasher to the brim and started it, I still had piles more to wash. I washed some more and put as many as would fit in the dish drainer. Then I took some bowls I'd cleaned and emptied the cat food into them.

Where were the cats hiding? I hoped they hadn't gotten out and run away. Or that I was wrong about them hiding out and surviving.

Judging by the litter pan, they'd been here very recently.

If I were a cat, I'd have retreated as far as I could from all the human activity. Carrying the bowls, I went upstairs. All the bedroom doors were open. Kelly's room and the bathroom were in disarray, but the kids' rooms seemed to be more or less in order. I called gently and was answered with a soft "mew" from Brianna's room. I stepped in and set the bowls on the floor.

Goddess, the mother cat, cautiously stuck her head out from under the bed. I pushed a bowl over toward her. She looked at me, then hesitantly crept out and sniffed the bowl. The two kittens followed her. I was surprised that they didn't seem any bigger than the last time I'd seen them, which was a few weeks ago. Hungrily, they all attacked the food.

I tried to ruffle Goddess's fur behind her ears, but she shied away from my hand. I left them alone to eat.

Scooping up food scraps, pizza boxes, and cigarette butts from all horizontal surfaces in the kitchen, including the floor, I filled several trash bags. I suppose I should have looked to see if there was recycling I should separate from the rest of it, but there was just so much *stuff*. And a lot of it was totally disgusting.

I carted a few bags of trash out to the garbage cans by the garage. A cold wet dusk was quickly turning into a freezing night. I figured I might as well sleep here, see what I could get done to get the place cleaned up and feed the cats again in the morning before I left. I'd stayed there often enough to know where Kelly kept things.

Then I tackled the cat litter pan. It was so disgustingly full I checked to make sure there was a supply of fresh litter, then emptied it completely into a sturdy trash bag. I scrubbed it out and dried it with a paper towel.

Then I filled it again, using the entire contents of the carton. Did that mean I should pick some up so Kelly wouldn't have to worry about it?

Staring at the living room, I decided that if I got the beer cans and bottles rinsed out and the trash picked up, I'd have a good part of it cleaned up.

An hour later it was back to looking something like a living room. Large bags of trash and recyclables lay next to the door. I wouldn't be able to do much about the damp spots in the rug—they smelled like beer, not vomit, at least, but I cleaned it as best I could, all the while remembering tales of people being electrocuted while operating vacuum cleaners on damp rugs. This time, that didn't happen.

I was just thinking about seeing if I could find anything to eat and maybe getting some sleep when the doorbell rang.

My first instinct was to ignore it and pretend that no one was in the house. But the lights were on and the front drapes were not tightly closed. Anybody on the front porch who peered through the cracks could see me.

I wiped my hands on my jeans and went to the door.

A man I didn't know stood there, his hair and clothes in disarray. He smelled of alcohol.

"Kelly here?" he asked.

"No." I wasn't about to offer any more information. "What do you need her for?"

He rocked back on his heels. "So you're the boyfriend, huh?"

I didn't see where that called for an answer.

He shrugged. "You and Kelly'll have to take the kids back," he said. "Louise fell and she can't take care of them right now. And my mother's not well enough. Her mind's gone. So they'll have to come stay here for now."

"Suppose she isn't able to?"

"Don't give me that. I called the hospital and she's been discharged. If she's been drinking, that's just too bad. It's her turn. I've been taking care of the kids for almost a week now."

I raised my eyebrows. "*You've* been taking care of the kids?"

"Well, me and my aunt and my mother. Definitely not Kelly."

That was true enough.

He turned toward the car parked at the curb and called, "Come on, kids, you're gonna stay with your mom for a while."

The door opened, and the two kids scrambled out, each clutching a backpack. They dashed up the sidewalk and onto the porch.

"Where's Mom?" Chris asked.

The man chuckled and swayed on his feet. "Probably passed out drunk."

The boy looked pained but didn't say anything.

Brianna launched herself across the threshold and leapt into my arms. "Jesse!" she sobbed, burying her face in my chest.

I wasn't sure what I should be doing, but I knew I wasn't going to leave the kids with this drunken fool, who I'd never met but was apparently their father. "Come on in," I said, putting my hand on Chris's shoulder and guiding him through the doorway. "Have you had supper?"

"No," he said in a small voice. "We've been riding around in Daddy's car, waiting for Mom to be home so we could come in."

The man nodded. "I saw the lights, and figured she's *finally* got home."

"Okay." I moved the kids and their stuff out of the doorway. "I'll see they're okay."

"You just do that." The man turned and stumbled down the porch steps toward the car.

He wasn't in any shape to drive, and I hoped he didn't get a DWI tonight. I knew he'd had at least one before, and if he got locked up for it, he wouldn't be working, and he wouldn't be making child support payments. Which Kelly needed.

Although another DWI and Kelly would have an easier time keeping custody.

"Where's Mom?" Chris asked again.

I looked at his drawn, worried face. The things kids have to go through. And they can't do a damn thing about it. These kids were no exception.

"She's out of the hospital," I said, "so she's getting better. But she had to go to someplace called a physical rehab 'cause she can't use her shoulder right, and they're gonna help her get better."

"Does she have to *sleep* there?" he asked.

"Probably."

He looked around the newly neatened living room. "Where's Pop-Pop and all his friends?"

I had to think a minute. PopPop must be Old Buckles. "He's gone on a trip," I said.

"Did his friends go, too?"

"I'm not sure. Probably some of them. But they're not staying here anymore." Not if I had anything to say about it.

He looked relieved. "Are you gonna stay with us?"

"I guess." The only alternative I could see would be to call child protective services. That would mean an emergency foster home. I'd at least stay with them tonight and see what I could figure out in the morning. Since the plant was closed down, I could stay with them for a few more days, too, if I had to.

We went into the kitchen, which was still pretty much a mess. Chris looked around. "Mom's not going to like this when she gets home," he said.

"That's why we're gonna clean it up as best we can," I said, setting Brianna in a chair by the table. "Let's see what we can find for supper."

The refrigerator held nothing but a tub of margarine, a half-empty bottle of catsup, and lots of beer. The freezer wasn't much better, but it did have some frozen vegetables.

A few cans and boxes, mostly soup and pasta, were on the pantry shelf. There was a half-empty jar of instant coffee and a few unopened packages of instant lemonade. I took some cans of vegetable soup and found a box of biscuit mix. That'd have to do for tonight. Tomorrow we'd have to go to the grocery store. I could barely afford to feed myself—how was I going to keep two kids fed, too?

While the biscuits were baking, we went upstairs and I helped the kids put the stuff from the backpacks away. Their extra clothes were clean. I knew we could thank Aunt Louise for that. I found spare sheets in the linen closet and stripped the used ones off their beds. Their rooms were not in disarray, but I had a queasy feeling that some people with less than perfect hygiene may very well have used the beds. And not only for sleeping.

We made the beds, then went on to Kelly's room. A funky odor told me her room had definitely been used for a variety of activities. I kicked the cans and greasy paper plates into the corner to tackle tomorrow. We changed those sheets, too, although I didn't think I quite dared sleep in her bed. The sofa in the living room would do fine for me.

Bundling the dirty sheets, we went back downstairs. I started the washing machine and dished out bowls of soup. The biscuits came out light and flaky. While I'd been in foster care with the Colemans, I'd learned the trick to fixing biscuits—handle the dough as little as possible. Their wonderful aroma filled the air and countered some of the stale stench that lingered.

"Do we have to go to school tomorrow?" Brianna asked.

School. I hadn't even thought about that. It'd be much easier to get to the store and finish cleaning up if the kids were in school. "Of course," I said. "Haven't you been going?"

"Not today," Chris said. "Aunt Louise has been driving us, but she didn't this morning."

"What happened to Aunt Louise?" I asked.

"She fell this morning, right down the stairs. She said she was okay, but she couldn't stand right. And she couldn't walk—she fell again. So she told me to call 9-1-1, then she went to sleep. Right there on the floor. An ambulance came, and they took her away."

"That's pretty grown up of you, to call 9-1-1 and get help like that," I said. "They didn't call anybody to take care of you? Or was your dad there?"

"They asked if anybody was home with us, and I told them Grandma."

Grandma was bedridden and suffering from dementia.

"Then what?"

"We just watched TV and waited until Daddy got home. Grandma never got out of bed. She doesn't, some days. We're not supposed to take food without asking, so we didn't have lunch. Or supper, until you fixed the soup."

"Well, we'll fix something for breakfast tomorrow. And I'll give you money for school lunches." That would put a dent in my available cash, but there wasn't much in the house I could give them, and they couldn't go to school with no lunch or lunch money.

While the kids finished up their meager supper, I emptied the dishwasher and put in a new load, including the supper dishes. The kitchen was beginning to look livable, too. It was a bit early for bedtime, so we went into the living room. The kids seemed happy to turn on the TV, and I was pretty tired, so I just sat with them on the couch as inane cartoon characters muddled their way through ludicrous situations. I never had a TV of my own, and I'd never watched the one in the dayroom on the cellblock much, so I wasn't too familiar with programming. This seemed terminally stupid.

Chris sat close to me, his tense muscles eventually relaxing. Brianna leaned her head on my arm and started to drift off to sleep.

"About time for bed," I said, pushing Brianna into a sitting position.

"We didn't do our homework," Chris said, avoiding my eyes. "We've had it for a week now."

"Why didn't you *tell* me you had homework?" I asked, exasperated. Stupid of me. I should have asked.

"My teacher's gonna be mad," Brianna said, rubbing her eyes.

"Why's she gonna be mad?" I asked.

"'Cause all my school stuff is over at Daddy's house."

Chris nodded. "And my books. So I *couldn't* do my homework."

"Maybe I can write a note and explain," I said. I didn't know if that would do any good. And would sending a note that I signed trigger some kind of investigation by the school system into the kids' living situation? It might.

I wasn't a parent. Or guardian. Was I opening myself to some kind of charges of interfering with lawful custody? Maybe kidnapping or unlawful restraint? Or even child abuse? I stirred uneasily. I wasn't sure how much the school knew about me, but whatever it was, it wasn't likely to be good.

The kids looked up at me trustingly. I knew I was going to take that chance.

"Will you read us bedtime stories?" Brianna asked.

"Yep. Get ready for bed. Teeth brushed and all. Then chose a book and I'll read it."

"Can we *each* choose a book?"

"I guess."

They scrambled upstairs.

I had to send Brianna back up to brush her hair. When she came down again, she was carrying Goddess the cat. The kittens tumbled down the stairs after her.

Finally we sat together on the sofa and opened the books. Brianna had *The Very Hungry Caterpillar* and Chris had *Are You My Mother*?

That seemed a bit babyish for him. I'm no psychologist, but I would have bet one could have made done a detailed report on that choice.

It was getting late, but I was in no hurry to finish reading. One kid cuddled close on each side of me, the cat lay on my lap purring, and the kittens batted playfully at the pages as I turned them.

A moment of joy and peace in a painful and uncertain world.

I was acutely aware of the huge empty feeling in my gut. This was probably the closest I was ever going to get to the life I'd missed out on by being locked up for all those years. Sometimes I could trick myself into thinking maybe Kelly and I had a future, but it was hard to think that now. *And what kind of a life could we have if she was always willing to believe the worst of me?* Besides, I reminded myself, I didn't have a hell of a lot to offer her and the kids. She'd be a fool to hook up her future with a paroled convict who could be whisked back to prison at a moment's notice. Especially one who was showing a real tendency to do stupid things and get in a lot of trouble.

We were just about finishing the second book when the front door swung open.

Kelly stood there, leaning against the doorframe and looking pale.

I sat frozen in astonishment and guilt.

"Mom!" Brianna cried, slipping off the sofa and rushing to her. She grabbed her mother's leg. Kelly swayed precariously.

I leapt to my feet, rushed over and grabbed Kelly to keep her from falling.

"What the hell are *you* doing here?" Kelly said to me, her words slurred.

I started to say I could have asked her the same thing, but after all she *lived* here. It was her house.

Leaning heavily on me, she made her way to the sofa and collapsed on it. The front door hung open behind us.

"Are you okay, Mom?" Chris asked, his eyes and voice panicky.

"No," she said.

The kids looked stricken.

"But I'm gonna be," she added.

"What happened?" Brianna asked.

"Damn rehab." Kelly struggled to sit upright. "Didn't do a damn thing for me. No exercise plan or nothing. Just wanted to give me drugs and have me stay in bed. Didn't pay no attention to nothing I said."

"How'd you get here from there?" I asked.

Her eyes were bloodshot, and she was still slurring her words. A thread of spittle drooled from the corner of her mouth. "Signed myself out. Took a cab. Cost me better'n forty bucks."

I looked at her in alarm. "Was that a good idea?"

"I don't care." She rubbed her eyes with the back of her hand. "We talked about no sleeping pills. They make me all groggy and sick, and I can't think straight. But they *don't* make me sleep. So they stopped giving them to me at the hospital. The rehab was supposed to get all the hospital records and do the same medication regime. So when they gave me some pills, I took them. And I didn't find out one was a sleeping pill until it was too late."

A chill wind blew through the open front door. I went over and shut it. "You want a cup of coffee or something?" I asked, remembering the instant in the pantry.

"No. I got to get to bed. I *know* that when I finally fall asleep I'm gonna sleep for fifteen hours and be sick when I wake up. But I need to sleep."

"Then let's get you up to bed," I said, glad we'd changed the sheets.

She peered at the kids. "I thought you were at your grandmother's. With Dad and Aunt Louise."

Clutching his book, Chris said, "Aunt Louise fell. And she went to the hospital."

"Chris had to call 9-1-1," Brianna chimed in. "An ambulance came. With its siren."

"Then when Dad came home, he said it was time for us to come stay with you."

"But there was nobody home, so we drove around for a while until there were lights on. And Jesse was here."

She looked up at me. "And *why* was Jesse here?"

I sighed. "Your dad gave me the key. Said he was taking off, and I had to come take care of the cats until you got out of rehab."

Shaking her head, she said, "It's way too late for you kids to be up. Let's all get to bed."

They looked at me. "Up to bed," I said. "Mom'll stop in to give good night kisses."

Reluctantly, they obeyed.

Careful of her sore shoulder, I helped Kelly up. She couldn't stand by herself. We inched up the stairs.

"I got to go to the bathroom," Kelly said, bracing her hand on the wall at the top of the stairs. "Can you help me?"

That didn't sound like something I wanted or ought to be doing, but I said, "I guess."

Fortunately, she could pull down her own pants with one hand, and she just needed me to lower her onto the seat. I waited outside until she called me to help her stand up, and once again she could handle her own pants as long as I held onto her so she didn't fall over.

Then I steadied her while she straightened Chris's bedding and bent down to give him a kiss on his forehead. He looked so lonely and scared. I reached over and grabbed a teddy bear from the dresser and tucked it in next to him. He clutched it tightly, and his eyes thanked me wordlessly.

Brianna cried and threw her arms around her mother's neck, which couldn't be good for her shoulder, so Kelly sat down on the bed and stroked her back to help her relax. In a few short minutes, Brianna's grip loosened, and she fell back on her pillow, asleep.

Kelly lurched to her feet and leaned heavily on me. We got to her bed, and she gingerly lay down. "I hate to ask you this, but could you get my shoes off?" she said.

Next to the request to help her go to the bathroom, pulling off the shoes was nothing. She was wearing a pair of loosely-tied sneakers. I unlaced them and pulled them off, then when she lay down, I tucked the covers around Kelly and moved to switch off the light.

"Wait a minute," she said, her voice cracking.

"Yeah?"

"Where are you going?"

Good question. "I was gonna stay overnight and get the kids on the school bus in the morning, but you're here now. So maybe I should just leave."

"Afraid your little girlfriend's gonna miss you?"

"Huh?"

"That sexy young blond you've been hanging around?"

"You mean Carissa?"

"If that's her name."

"She's a reporter for the *Rothsburg Register*."

"Pretty glamorous."

"That's not what I mean. She's been trying to get a story."

"About you?"

"Sometimes. But mostly about the Predators."

"They wouldn't be too happy about that."

"True, that."

"So you're not seeing her?"

"Not as in going out with her. Besides, she's got a boyfriend now."

"Yeah? Anybody I know?"

I shook my head. "You know Detective Belkins?"

Kelly started to snort, but it turned into a painful cough. Finally she said, "You mean that plainclothes cop that's been harassing you?"

I wasn't sure 'harassing' was the right word, but she had the right cop. "Yeah. That one."

"Unbelievable."

"I was surprised myself."

Kelly rolled over and shielded her eyes from the light. "But I guess it means she won't be trying to get you in bed with her."

I wasn't so sure about that, but I was sure I wouldn't be taking her up on it if she did offer.

"Then do you think you could stay overnight?" Kelly asked. "And get the kids off to school? I'm afraid I won't be able to wake up in time."

It would save me a cold, wet walk across town. And she might not be able to get the kids off herself in the morning. They shouldn't be missing any more school if we could help it. "If you want me to," I said. "But I thought you were mad at me."

"I was. And I'm sorry. Turns out Black Rose was lying."

"About me telling Razorback he could have a go at you?"

"Yeah. And about you screwing her."

I couldn't help but ask, "How'd you figure that out?"

"When they found Razorback's body buried at that construction site."

Montgomery had told me about that, but I wanted to know what she knew. And how she felt about it. "What do you mean?"

"Black Rose said he'd taken off when he realized he was gonna be picked up for rape. He'd managed to keep from getting in trouble for the last few years, but this was for sure gonna violate his parole."

I nodded. Once someone makes the sex offenders' registry, getting parole violated is pretty easy. Especially for new skin charges.

Kelly rubbed her shoulder. Her eyes looked heavy. "He knew he'd get locked up if he stuck around. If he survived when my dad found him. Or if he ever came back. So he cleaned out their bank account and planned to take off."

"The money they'd been saving for new equipment?"

"Yeah. And their operating capital. That made Rose *really* mad."

I was pretty sure I knew, but I asked, "So what did she do?"

Kelly looked up at me like I was stupid. "She *killed* him. And then she loaded his body on the trailer along with the backhoe and hauled it out to the construction site and buried it."

I didn't think Old Buckles had an opportunity to talk to Kelly about any of this before he took off. Had she figured that out on her own?

"If Black Rose'd had a better handle on how the storm water drainage was supposed to work, they'd probably never have found him. But the inspector had a fit when she saw how the contour was changed and insisted they redo it."

She'd been talking to *someone.* "Who told you all that?"

"Li'l Mama. She was all bent out of shape. Black Rose has been her running buddy for years."

"So that's why he didn't take his bike. It was still parked by the backhoe up at the excavating company lot."

Kelly closed her eyes. "Yep. Black Rose tried to say he thought it was too conspicuous for him to ride if he was trying to avoid being arrested, but I've never known a biker who didn't think he could outrun the law on his bike. At least for a while."

I thought about Old Buckles on his trike. He had no illusions that it would be long before he was caught, but he rode it anyhow. "Your dad's taken off," I said.

She sighed. "I'm not surprised. It won't be too long before they pick him. I actually think at this point in his life he's more comfortable locked up. I'll just put his trike in the garage and go visit him in prison every month. Like I've always done." Her words slurring worse, and her eyes were drooping closed.

"If you can get to sleep, you'd better take advantage of it," I said, reaching for the light switch again.

"You gonna be here when I wake up?" she asked. I could come up with so many reasons why that wouldn't be a good idea. It wouldn't be long before something else came up and she jumped to the worst possible conclusion about me. She still drank too much—I was being an enabler. The kids were beginning to care about me much too much. Odds were the whole thing wouldn't work out long term between Kelly and me, and it would just hurt them that much more if I suddenly disappeared.

I looked at Kelly snuggled in her warm bed and thought about the times she'd invited me to share it. And about how it felt to fix supper for the kids and sit with them, reading stories at bedtime. Things I had no right to expect to ever happen in my life.

From down the hallway, Brianna's voice called, "Jesse, my blankets came off! Can you come tuck me in again?"

Kelly was waiting for an answer. "I'll be here if you want me to," I said.

ABOUT THE AUTHOR

KM Rockwood has a diverse background including working as a laborer in a steel fabrication plant, operating glass melters and related equipment in a fiberglass manufacturing facility, and supervising an inmate work crew in a large medium security state prison. These jobs, as well as work as a special education teacher in an alternative high school and a GED teacher in county detention facilities, provide most of the basis for novels and short stories.

Look for upcoming books in the Jesse Damon series, including: *The Buried Biker*, *Sendoff for a Snitch*, and *Brothers in Crime*.

www.kmrockwood.com

www.ingramcontent.com/pod-product-compliance
Lightning Source LLC
Chambersburg PA
CBHW050750250626
47155CB00005B/1999